Esben Laursen

Dissension

DISSENSION

Forlag/Publishing House: *BoD · Books on Demand GmbH, In de Tarpen 42, 22848 Norderstedt, Tyskland*

Tryk/Print: Libri Plureos GmbH, Friedensallee 273, 22763 Hamborg, Tyskland

ISBN: 978-87-4305-898-4

Esben Laursen

Dissension

"I can resist anything except temptation."

– Oscar Wilde: *Lady Windermere's fan*

Chapter one
Johnny Roy Smith

It had been one of those pleasant New York spring days when the temperatures range from forty Fahrenheit in the early morning, to near seventy Fahrenheit in the afternoon, and then it gets chilly again in the late evening. It almost feels like the afternoon is a day in itself; an entity of its own, during which you tend to think that the winter is definitely over.

Now, at dusk, Johnny Roy Smith is lustful and high on life. He's had a pleasant day consisting of a light breakfast followed by a morning run and a thirty-minute full body workout. After that, he indulged himself with a printed version of the *Washington Times*, a stroll through Hell's Kitchen, and a quick meal followed by three beers. It took him only a little more than an hour to gulp down the beers, and he strategically spent this time in the sun to improve his tan before nighttime. Upon returning to the hotel, he took a nap and afterwards a long shower. He resisted the urge to masturbate in the shower cabin, but it was a struggle; his fantasies and impulses almost got the better of him.

After sunset, when he leaves the hotel, the mild afternoon breeze seems a distant memory, and he pulls up his collar and quickens his pace, as if attempting to outrun the chilliness. He senses that it might be just a minute away from raining, which is one more reason to move quicker—messy hair would be a disadvantage—and finds comfort in knowing that in less than ten minutes he'll be at Connolly's Pub.

As always, the pub is packed, and he quickly scans the premises as soon as he's inside. The in-house singer-songwriter must have left the stage, as the back-drop tunes come from music-videos on TV screens scattered around the pub. He knows from previous experiences that they are tuned into a channel which doesn't play up-to date-music; tonight, during his first ten minutes in the pub, he sees Chris Martin jumping around in circles, Nicki Minaj being pissed off, and then Mark Knopfler does "Walk of Life", which is not an awful song, but it seems weird that it's still played in 2024. Following this, the Weeknd really lets Connolly's Pub know that it is the weekend: "I said, ooh, I'm blinded by the lights, no, I can't sleep until I feel your touch." Not a new song, but not totally outdated either, he thinks, as he notices how the party around him kicks into a higher gear. Shortly after, his inner voice instinctively reminds him that he didn't come for the music, and he turns his attention to the bar as he begins to zoom in on the female clientele.

It doesn't take long before he approaches a woman; she's not the first one he has laid eyes on when scanning the bar, but over the years he has become pragmatic about his choices. Out of the roughly twenty-five women in the bar, she's far from the prettiest one, but he knows that approaching one of the prettier fe-males will likely be a waste of his and her time; it will set him back an hour, and he might not have that much time to spare. He moves closer to his prey and becomes pleasantly surprised as he realizes that she's better looking than his initial impression from twenty-five feet away made him believe; calling her *pretty* would be pushing it, but she's not ugly; fifteen years ago, she was a real knockout, he thinks, and time has treated her relatively kindly. He can still make out beautiful features in her face: a symmetric nose, large eyes, full lips, and a smooth forehead, which, despite her age, of perhaps forty, displays hardly any blemishes or wrinkles. On this night, for Johnny Roy Smith, who sees himself as a good-looking, middle-aged man, this somewhat attractive lady is an obvious choice; a typical plan-A girl. Johnny is conveniently unaware of the fact that he's merely an average-looking man, feels overly confident from the get-go, and also reassures himself that not jacking off earlier was definitely the right decision. Upon striking up a conversation with the relatively attractive woman, it doesn't take long for Johnny to conclude that he's probably not wasting his time here; she soon begins to lean towards him, twirling her hair, as if obviously drawing attention to her psychical appearance, and she smiles and laughs frequently at whatever he says.

It has taken Johnny a while to identify the *modus operandi* that produces the highest probability of seducing a plan-A girl. New York is his go-to-city, but he quickly learned that Brooklyn girls were not impressed by his appearance. Despite an expensive shirt, a shiny watch and plenty of fancy jewelry, they tended to find him coarse; not necessarily a poor man in a rich man's shirt, but a somewhat unclassy man. Queens girls were too exotic for him; not in the sense that *he* had anything against *them*, but because his whiteness was a thorn in their side, an unwelcome reminder that he was more privileged. It was the same, maybe even worse, with Bronx girls; to them he was an outright enemy.

He had tried chatting up non-Caucasian girls plenty of times, and though some evenings hadn't been a complete crash-and-burn, he's had so many one-way-conversations and brush-offs that he knows that if he really wants to improve his chances of getting laid, then a Caucasian, middle-aged, moderately attractive and quite drunk woman is his safest bet. Sometimes he had tried his luck on Staten Island or in New Jersey, because he knew that there were plenty of white women in their forties there, but he didn't like the public transportation to those places, and he'd also had quite a few swing-and-miss-nights there, so eventually Times Square, a place he otherwise resented, had become his favorite picking-up-girls location.

Times Square, despite its lack of charm, had proven to come with a number of benefits. First of all, it was easy to get there, as he didn't have to bother with other transportation following the seventy-seven-minute MNR train ride. Secondly, the bars were lined up like pearls on a string, and if the first bar proved to be a bad choice, then the next bar was likely to be less than a minute away. The greatest advantage of Times Square, however, was the hordes of tourists, from all over the world, who went there and let their guard down. Of course, tourists came in all kinds of sizes and shapes, and some of the women were too old for him, whereas some were too young. Plenty of them were also too ugly for his taste, while others were out of his league, and many women visited New York with their husbands and would never dream of spending time with him, nor would they be allowed to. Finally, and this had also happened to him, a considerable number of foreign women were not into him, because they were into other women. However, with the logic of a mathematician, Johnny had spent the past two decades arriving at the conclusion that if a white, preferably European, middle-aged woman was at Connolly's Pub in Times Square, either alone or with friends, then there was, after all, a good chance that she was susceptible to his charm and that she was either looking for an adventure, or could be convinced that she needed one.

Times Square was crowded, noisy, and too touristy, but eventually he taught himself to grin and bear it. Every time he went there, he taught himself to turn a blind eye to how annoying it was that the tourists walked so slowly because they looked at all the neon signs, ignored none of the panhandlers, stared numbly into the sky, as if they didn't have skyscrapers in their own countries, and beheld the beggars with a strange, oxymoronic mix of empathy and indifference. They also took pictures of buildings, bars, restaurants, police officers, taxis, street signs, posters, hot dog vendors, firemen, fire hoses, billboards—whatever they considered *typically New York*—and they always walked besides each other, never behind or in front of each other, thereby forcing everyone behind them to slow down. But, as soon as Johnny had taught himself to pay no attention to all of this, he realized that the one advantage of Times Square, female tourists, outweighed all the disadvantages and going there was the means to his end. In terms of being on the prowl, Johnny's conclusion was that he didn't stand a better chance in any other bar anywhere in New York, or anywhere else for that matter.

Following this eye-opener, Johnny Roy Smith developed a specific set of questions that were good at initiating a conversation with your average Barbara from Germany or Martina from Spain. The obligatory where-are-you-from question preceded all other questions, of course, and it paved the way for a list of inquiries. How do you like New York? How long have you been here? Is this your first time in New York? How long are you planning on spending in New York? What have you seen here? What's your favorite part of New York? How do you like New Yorkers? Although these questions seemed trivial, they not only served the purpose of establishing a connection but they also allowed Johnny to commence the process of positioning himself as next day's tour guide for the venturesome tourist, telling her how she of course *did* have to see Central Park, Columbus Circle, The Flatiron Building, High Line Park, the Vessel, Rockefeller Center, Empire State Building, The World Trade Center Memorial, and Chelsea Market. He would also tell her that hopping on the Statue of Liberty ferry and walking across Brooklyn Bridge are must-dos. However, it was also important, and at this point he would lean closer to her, that she experienced the *real* New York; *his* city, all the places where the tourists rarely went.

He would then begin his tale about how much time he had spent in New York during his thirty-six years (in truth he was forty-one) and how much he still enjoyed visiting the city. Initially, he would talk about his upbringing in Hoboken and the frequent trips to

Manhattan with his parents during his formative years. Then he would talk about the teenage journeys with his friends where they would go shopping in SoHo or catch a movie in the Alamo on Liberty Street. Later, his friends and he would start going out for drinks, not only in Manhattan, but also in Brooklyn and Queens, and sometimes their nightly excursions would even take them all the way to the Bronx. Subsequently, he would share all the details about how his fascination with New York would take him as far as the Park Slope apartment where he spent almost five years. The final part was talking about how his parents in the meantime had left Hoboken and settled in the quaint, little village of Cold Spring because Henry, his father, wanted to pursue his passion for hiking and hunting.

Unfortunately, his parents had spent less than a year in Cold Spring before they urged him to come by one afternoon because Evelyn, his mother, had something to share with him. Due to the tone in her voice, he knew right away that it was bad news and the seventy-seven minutes' commute was spent anxiously awaiting *how* bad the news was. When his mother told him that it was sclerosis he immediately knew that it would be a matter of a few months, certainly less than a year, before he would uproot and move to Cold Spring as well. The hustle and bustle of New York City was beginning to feel tiresome to him, but the main argument was that he needed to be near his mother; his father was the stronger of his parents, whereas he was certain that the sickness would quickly take its toll on his mother, who had always been a frail weakling. Today, fifteen years after the diagnosis, Evelyn was still alive, but she was crippled and almost entirely paralyzed, and had spent the last five years either in her bed or in a wheelchair. In other words, his suspicion had proven right; her health had deteriorated more rapidly and aggressively than what would have been the case for your average sclerosis patient, and he had never regretted moving closer to her. At last, Johnny would end his tale with an enough-about-me-and-my-family comment and pass the conversation over to his female choice of the night.

Everything in Johnny's eyes and body language oozed sincerity as he told women these things. He was always aware of appearing as trustworthy as possible and reminded himself how good he was at just that before he embarked on one of his nightly outings; a lie detector couldn't catch any of my lies, he thought. He had heard that if you tell a lie plenty of times, sooner or later you start to believe that it's true and this might have happened to him. It was not that every single detail in his story was a lie; he *did* live in Cold Spring and his mother *was* alive, and the depiction of her as a frailer person than his father wasn't entirely untrue, although dainty might be a more accurate word to assign her. She was *not* a sclerosis patient, however, and, apart from a few bodily defects that were perfectly normal for a woman her age, she was in great shape in every possible way. Growing up in Hoboken was also a lie, and so were the stories about the recurring trips to New York. In fact, he had never once crossed the Hudson River. Johnny was born and raised in Cold Spring, had spent thirty-six of his forty-one years there, and was brought up on heartland rock. He was a village boy; provincial, laid-back and to some extent one-dimensional. It was true that he had spent five years in a Park Slope apartment, and it was also accurate that he still enjoyed visiting the great metropolis, but he didn't "have New York in his blood", as he liked to phrase it, and he had felt a sigh of relief after he left the city and moved back home.

It had taken him a number of years before he felt that he had nailed this life-story and managed to turn it into one that was perfectly construed to seduce women; initially, he hadn't lied about his job, but at some point it became evident that the truth, being a salesman who worked for Smith's Carmarket, his father's used car dealership, did not work in his favor. While he could truthfully claim that he was good at his job and was sure to take over the business someday, salesmen were seen as slick and shallow, and since these adjectives were fitting descriptions of him, and since he knew that he did have a tendency to come across as a too-clever-by-half type, there was no need to add to this image by confessing to his actual profession.

Therefore, on some nights, Johnny had been a firefighter, on other occasions he had been a paramedic, and he had also tried being a police officer; professions which were all defined by the heroic willingness and ability to save people. Two years ago, he decided that he would stick to the valiant police-officer persona, not because it was necessarily better than being a paramedic or a firefighter, but simply because he needed some consistency in his deceit; it was easier and probably more convincing to stick to the same lie every time. In addition to that, he was also acquainted with a couple of officers of the law, so although he knew something about a fireman's or a paramedic's job, he knew more about a police officer's line of duty.

Everything in Johnny's made-up narrative was created by his own imagination, except on one occasion, when he was given a "helping hand" by a thirty-five-year-old lady from Amsterdam. In Connolly's Pub, sometime around September 2021, Johnny had offered Judith a drink, which she had willingly accepted, whereupon they exchanged stories about his "upbringing in Hoboken" and her upbringing in a Dutch village. When he got to the part where he told her about moving back to Cold Spring to be closer to his parents, she asked him if they had any severe diseases. He was taken aback by the frankness in her question but managed to analyze the situation in a split-second and answered "yes" to a question which rightfully should have been answered with a "no".

It could've been a coincidence, of course, she could've just been one horny Dutchwoman, and the night might have ended the same way even without his little lie, but the fact of the matter was that he did end up screwing her brains out less than three hours after he affirmed her question, and they did it again in the morning, slightly less aggressively this time, and at least five more times in the remaining three nights she spent in New York.

On more than one occasion, Judith would return to her praise of the *caring* and *self-sacrificing* son who left a good job and a great apartment in New York City to take care of his mother who lived in a tiny, quiet village, so maybe that little plot-twist wasn't so insignificant after all; a man of twenty-six who leaves New York

City behind to move closer to his mother in Cold Spring is a mommy's boy–which most women find unsexy– whereas a man of twenty-six who leaves New York City behind to move closer to his *sick* mother in Cold Spring is a caring, affectionate and empathetic man–which most women find sexy–so from time to time he reminds himself to send a kind thought to Judith from Holland for providing his narrative with just one more detail which in all probability has made it easier for him to lure women into his trap.

Over the years, Johnny has made a habit of keeping accurate track of the number of women that have been unable to resist him: Since moving to Cold Spring fifteen years ago, tonight is his seventy-second trip to New York and in the preceding seventy-one trips he has had sex with Agnes and Anniken from Norway; Fransisca, Valeria, and Rosa from Spain; Claudia and Elena from Switzerland; Helmi from Finland; Mila from Belgium; Sophia and Mia from Germany; Lucia from Chile; Celine from France (technically, they didn't have sex, because he couldn't get an erection); Zoe and Judith from Holland; Elsa and Frideborg from Sweden; Susanne from Denmark; Khrystyna from Ukraine (a bad experience; after he fucked her, she cried over the loss of her husband, who was killed by Putin's soldiers); Nélida from Argentina; and four English members of the fair sex: Zara, Raleigh, and Eleanor from London, two of whom he actually managed to seduce during the same weekend, and Willow from Brighton.

All in all, Johnny is satisfied with his track record. He has decided that Celine still counts, because the art of seduction is almost as important to him as the sex itself. Ideally, he would like to reduce the overrepresentation of European women, but it's a result of his pragmatic approach; for him, Europeans are simply easier to get in the sack as he's aligned with them. They are the plan-A girls, and only if this plan fails does Johnny consider resorting to plan B, which is a walk to the local ATM machine, followed by a subway ride to Roosevelt Avenue in the Corona neighborhood of Queens, the so-called "Market of Sweethearts".

Plan B, which he has resorted to exactly 16 times over the years, isn't entirely bad, he thinks, as it provides him with the opportunity of handpicking exotic girls. In recent years, Johnny has sent Greg Abbot a kind thought, as he's responsible for sending thousands of Venezuelan asylum seekers north after crossing the US-Mexico border and some of them end up in miniskirts and tight tops on Roosevelt Avenue.

Thank God for conservative, southern governors, he has thought, and laughed at his own joke. Another thing Johnny likes about plan B is that he can convince himself that it isn't really a plan B; despite the fact that he has to pay the Roosevelt Avenue girls at least one hundred dollars, he somehow manages to make himself believe that in *his* case they don't necessarily do it for the money, because it's nice for them to be with a costumer who's as young, well-groomed, and handsome as him.

Little does Johnny know that he's wrong about this; it's a fucking job for them—nothing else; to them he's just as reprehensible as the costumer before and the one after.

Withdrawing money from an ATM is nothing Johnny has to worry about on this lovely New York spring evening, as he aims to get lucky with this not-unattractive, fortyish woman in Connolly's Pub. Though he's less than half an hour into his visit to the pub, he's already feeling confident that his plan-A girl for the night, Sarah from Manchester, will be susceptible to his charm. One drink becomes two drinks and two drinks become four drinks and when she tells him that she's forty-seven, this is her last night in New York, and she's on her own because her friends have stayed in the hotel due to mix of being overwhelmed, tired, and hung-over from the five nights they've spent in New York so far, he's guessing that she will be in his hotel room in less than an hour. Had she been a forty-seven-year-old woman who looked seven years older, he probably would have lost his interest, unless he had been really drunk, but since this is a forty-seven-year-old who looks seven years younger, the situation is more or less optimal for him. Had she really been forty, she probably would have been a little less desperate than what is now the case, but this one is a done deal, he thinks. There are some vague indications that suggest Sarah is married: the skin on her index finger has a paler band, as though she normally wears a ring, which is one indication, and her tendency to tilt the phone away from him when she's texting is another—but there are more signs that show she doesn't care about that tonight. The sappy-sick-mother story seals the deal and Johnny's intuition proves right; fifty-five minutes after he was certain that she would be at his hotel in less than an hour, that's exactly where she is, and ten minutes after opening the door to his room, he slides his dick into her perfectly shaved, middle-aged, Manchester pussy for the first time. Then they sleep for a few hours, whereupon they repeat the act, and when she leaves his hotel room after that, he pats himself on the back for having banged no less than five ladies from England in recent years. "Oh, oh, I'm a horny bitch, I'm a really horny bitch, I'm an Englishwoman in New York," he sings to himself and thinks that if he were ever to leave the States, moving to England wouldn't be a bad idea. He then checks the time, realizes that he doesn't have to leave for another three hours, and decides to catch at least one more hour's sleep. He feels on top of the world right now and becomes drowsy as he contemplates the idea that the last five or six years have really started to turn him into the badass that he was born to be. Though he can no longer pick and choose women—he never really could, but likes to think of his past in that way—he's still good at picking up women. If he continues to stick to his carefully planned strategy, then he can likely continue to be a womanizer for another twenty years, possibly even longer than that. That seems like a long time, almost like a lifetime; there's something infinite about it, he thinks; infinite blowjobs, hand-jobs and tit-jobs, and infinite pussy. This is what his future will hold; an adventurous and hedonistic life, with years to come that are just as promising as those passed.

Chapter two
Alicia Clare Vanderbilt

It's just past midnight when the dial tone of Alicia Clare Vanderbilt's iPhone pulls her out of her sleep. She's not used to being woken up by her phone and is disoriented as she tries to locate it. It must be one of the kids, she thinks, right before finding the phone below the pillow, so she becomes even more perplexed as she sees *his* name on the display. Her husband is not in the habit of calling her after bedtime when he's out of town, which makes her worry that something must have happened. She mumbles an indistinct combination of "yeah" and "hello" into the phone. When no one answers her muffled voice, she clears her throat and speaks up, only to realize that there's still no response on the other end of the line. Following this, she says "hello" a few times, each time more loudly, but starts to consider hanging up as everything she says goes unanswered. It must be a pocket call, she concludes, and is just about to hang up when she hears voices on the other end. Though the chatter is indistinct, there's no mistaking that one voice belongs to her husband and the other belongs to a woman. Initially, Alicia thinks that he has been in an accident, but quickly she shuns the thought as there's no surrounding noise. There are two voices and nothing else, which must mean that he's not on the *streets* of New York. She wonders whether he could be in a hospital, but also considers this unrealistic because of the complete silence that seemingly surrounds her husband and this woman. Had he been in a hospital there would be other sounds, such as ringing phones, audio announcements, bleeping monitors, alarms, and blaring televisions, and there would also be the sound of pain; women retching, men yelling, or babies crying. A hospital is never completely silent.

Alicia has become silent and is instead trying to zoom in on the content of the conversation. However, the distance between the phone and those not speaking into it is so great that she cannot make out the words, despite desperately pushing the button on the side of her phone to adjust the volume and pressing her ear as close to the screen as possible. Again, she considers hanging up, but ends up putting the phone down as she also has to go to the bathroom. When she returns to the bedroom, she picks up the phone and quickly learns that there's no longer a conversation on the other end of the line. Instead of inaudible words, Alicia now hears *sounds*. To begin with, they are somewhat indistinguishable, but she slowly starts to realize what she's listening to; kissing lips, groping hands, bodies rolling around on a bed, and sonorous moans. The sounds are no longer difficult to identify and it's no longer possible to misapprehend the situation, as it's now the most universal sound in the world that is relayed to Alicia; the sound of sex. Her fucking husband is going at it with some slut and though Alicia would prefer not to suffer the indignity of overhearing this, she finds it impossible to hang up, and ends up listening to the entire intercourse—it lasts almost half an hour—which is far longer than what she has been used to when she, on rare occasions, has had sex with her husband in recent years. Alicia goes to the bathroom one more time to check herself in the mirror as if wanting to confirm that she really *is* awake and that she's not in the midst of a nightmare. Thereafter, she picks up her phone again and hears how the gasping sounds have come to an end and are replaced by the sound of her snoring husband. In some bizarre way she finds listening to this just as humiliating as listening to their fornication, and she finally manages to hang up and retreat to the kitchen.

The first thing Alicia does is grab a beer from the fridge. She doesn't drink a lot and certainly not by herself in the middle of the night, but realizes that she needs a drink to remain composed; she's a second away from screaming and swearing and is overwhelmed by an urge to pick up any piece of silverware and hurl it against the wall. An inner voice manages to convince her that she mustn't do anything to wake up the kids, and she succeeds in retreating to a chair and calming herself to the point where she's able to surrender to somewhat silent tears. She cries and cries and cries. She cries like a baby that doesn't know where its parents are. At times she's able to stop crying for a little while, but then the tears find their way to her eyes again. At one point she tries to get up, but her legs are trembling as much as her body and she's unable to carry her own weight, so she lies on the floor and cries some more. Though no one is watching, she hides her face in the palms of her hands and continues to weep for more than two hours, until eventually snot drips from her nose, and snot and tears combine to form one liquid mass that covers her entire lower face.

When she stands up, she notices their weekly family calendar: April 6, 2024. Under any other circumstances, a beautiful date; the beginning of spring; her favorite season of the year. But right now, the only thing she can focus on are the two words in her husband's section for this particular weekend: New York. Once she has stared at these words for what feels like an eternity, she flips several pages backwards and realizes that the same two words were also written in her husband's section six and nine weeks ago. She then notices that this year's calendar is placed in front of last year's, which for some reason hasn't been thrown out, and she decides to flip through the 2023 calendar, leaving her in a state of sheer panic when she realizes that her husband spent eight weekends in New York last year. It takes Alicia less than a second to conclude that he's having an affair; she's convinced that her husband checks into a hotel with his mistress every time he goes to New York. While she has no idea what the other woman looks like, her mind very easily conjures up images of women of different shapes, sizes, and colors. First, Alicia imagines her husband with a twenty-year-old, big-tittied lover, then with a thirty-year-old, big-bootied lover. Subsequently, she imagines him with a forty-year-old lover, whose body is a replica of her own, but eventually realizes that all images leave her with the same torturous feeling, so she does her best to shun them, goes back upstairs, telling herself that she should try to get a couple of hours' sleep before the kids wake up, or at least try to get her mind on something else.

Alicia quickly learns that the bed offers no consolation; in fact, it only reminds her even more of *him*. His scent is in the sheets, and though she never misses him while he's out of town, his absence now is a poignant reminder of the feelings that at least *used* to be between them. Instead of falling asleep, her mind starts to take her through their entire relationship, starting with the memory of how they met almost twenty years ago, when she was on one of her rare nights of barhopping. She has never been particularly fond of drinking because she doesn't like the loss of control that comes with alcohol consumption, and, at the time, also considered being drunk or hungover a waste of time. An occasional glass of champagne or chardonnay was alright, but that was usually as far as it went for Alicia Clare Vanderbilt back then. Being a freshman at Yale Law School, she was exceedingly devoted to her studies, and leisure time was scarce, yet on this night, May 8, 2004, she had decided to join a group of fellow Yale students who were going to New York for drinks. Initially, she hadn't really been up for it, as the others were setting themselves up for a crazy night, and she had only been drunk a handful of times and being drunk in *New York* frightened her.

But, she had recently turned twenty-one, and, having declined other invitations, was running out of valid excuses, and maybe, just maybe, somewhere buried deep down inside of her, there was a longing to do it; a budding desire to cut loose, just once, and see where her instincts would take her. For as long as she could remember, she had always done the right thing; her nose had been buried in schoolbooks for what felt like an eternity, she invested herself in dozens of extracurricular activities, took piano lessons and ballet lessons, excelled in showjumping, and never once questioned whether she was doing what *she* wanted, or what her *parents* wanted. Undoubtedly, she was born with a silver spoon in her mouth, which offered plenty of advantages, but also plenty of expectations. She was hardly a teenager before the when-you-get-into-Yale talk became a weekly thing, and when she left Fairfield County to move to Harkness Hall she wasn't a facsimile of her parents, but she was definitely a product of her upbringing. She had lived in three different houses in Fairfield County, each one bigger and more expensive than the previous one, and the Alicia Clare Vanderbilt who enrolled in Yale was an upper-class, privileged, and ambitious young woman, with a fondness for "the Establishment", which she was on her way to becoming a part of. One night out wouldn't impair this image, and she had decided that bending the elbow a bit would be alright; come Sunday evening she would be back at her book-filled desk and she was determined to let Saturday evening be a short, but welcome, distraction from constitutional law, criminal law, civil procedure, and contracts.

It was four o'clock in the afternoon and the five YLS students were already tipsy as they boarded the New Haven train bound for Times Square. During the train ride, their conversation was more unrestrained than usual and during a what's-your-number chat, Alicia had to confess that she was virtually a virgin; she came very close to sleeping with her high school prom date, but vaginal pain prevented it from happening, so she didn't know if that *counted,* and certainly felt younger than her age, when she realized that she didn't have other stories to share. "Get drunk and get it done," was their advice for the night, and luckily she didn't have to respond to this proposition, which she found a bit frightening, before it was someone else's turn to share (s)experiences. In New York they found a bar and Alicia, who was now inebriated, quickly noticed one of the bartenders, who was wearing a name tag that said Johnny. Eventually, he noticed her noticing him, and, being far less shy than her, initiated a conversation. Following this, he approached her every time he could take a minute off his bartending chores, which amounted to seven times until midnight, by which time he was off duty. Upon this, Alicia and Johnny spent a few hours exchanging life-stories, jokes and kisses, and one thing led to another, until suddenly she found herself in his Park Slope apartment and there was no doubt this time; whatever virginity she may have had left was gone by the time she left his apartment the day after. In the following two months, she visited him three times, despite the fact that she wasn't sure that he was her type. Johnny seemed to live from hand to mouth; he was either working or drinking, or combining the two. He had finished high school with a mediocre GPA and apparently had no ambitions to go to college at any time. He was in many ways her complete opposite, but YLS-life was strenuous, and she had to admit that she felt rejuvenated every time she spent a couple of nights with him. She was determined to finish law school, but New Haven wasn't new heaven, and having a sex-life for the first time in her life made Alicia feel more like a woman. A little bit of dick every now and then to take the edge off things wasn't a bad idea; after all, she wasn't thinking about marrying this guy, so she spent the next three months visiting him five times and before she knew it, and certainly before she had planned it, or had even touched upon the issue with him, she was one month into her pregnancy.

At the onset of her pregnancy, Alicia was determined to continue her studies, but in time she realized that giving birth to twins, who beheld the world for the first time in July 2005, meant having to quit Yale. In the meantime, she had moved into Johnny's Park Slope apartment, and they spent a few good years there, before they agreed on moving to Cold Spring. Alicia was used to provincial life, but she wasn't used to provincial life with children, and Johnny often worked long hours, so she spent a lot of time by herself, and when the kids started elementary school, the TV was just as often her sole companion as any of her family members. By now the children were old enough to engage in play dates and leisure activities, but not so old that Alicia had the freedom to travel or go on extended family visits. As a result of this, she was often more than just alone; she was *lonely*.

In addition, the differences between Johnny and herself were becoming increasingly evident; they often joked about having to put up a *no politics, no religion* sign on the fridge, and while being able to joke about it was a good thing, it was undeniable that they were the embodiments of two very different types of Americans, and their relationship gradually became more fragile. Every so often, Alicia did consider leaving Johnny, but she always concluded that the advantages of staying married would be greater than the disadvantages of getting a divorce; though she could probably live without *him*, surely breaking up would be a devastating blow for the kids, and despite the fact that Johnny often toiled away at work, she had to admit that he didn't neglect his duties around the house, when he was there, nor was he a negligent father. Had she left him in favor of life as a single mom, there would never be anyone else than her to empty the dishwasher, mow the lawn, wash the clothes, take out the trash, bathe the kids, cook their meals, wipe their noses and butts, put BAND-AIDS on scraped knees, vacuum the house, defrost the fridge, wash the windows, dust the shutters, and clean the carpets. The thought of becoming a one-woman army was so overwhelming that she, instead of leaving the fellow, agreed to marry him when he proposed in the summer of 2007.

Planning their wedding offered plenty of opportunities to focus on the good things in their relationship, and the months before and after their wedding were probably the happiest period they ever shared. Likewise, most things went according to plan on the actual wedding day and Alicia generally remembers this day as one of the highlights of her adult life. Some guests were surprised to learn that neither Alicia nor Johnny took the other's last name; they had gone over different combinations: Alicia Clare Smith. Alicia Smith-Vanderbilt. Johnny Vanderbilt. Johnny Roy-Vanderbilt. Johnny Smith Vanderbilt. None of them *sounded right*, and eventually they discarded the idea of becoming the Smiths or the Vanderbilts. What's in a name? Alicia thought, but never shared the joke with Johnny, as she was certain he wouldn't get the reference, so they simply told each other that not taking each other's names was a non-issue. After they were joined in holy matrimony, the years came and went, and as the kids were growing up, Alicia managed to find a new path for herself. She realized that she would never pass the bar and instead became a legal assistant, a job which helped sustain her interest in law while still leaving her with enough time to attend to her motherly duties and feelings. She watched her twins grow up to become wholesome children and now, as they are pushing towards the end of their teenage years, she acknowledges that growing up in today's America isn't the easiest thing, but is no more worried about them than your average parent. She looks forward to guiding them through the final furlong into adulthood, and although their son tends to be a mommy's boy and their daughter tends to be a daddy's girl, she believes that she will maintain a healthy relationship with them when they someday leave the house and wander off into the world.

As Alicia approaches the end of her involuntary trip down memory lane, she ponders the fact that, although her marriage had been far from perfect, Johnny cheating on her is something she hadn't seen coming; obviously there were red flags in their relationship, but since they hadn't talked about getting a divorce in recent years, she figured that they had somehow silently agreed that even if the bond between them wasn't particularly romantic, at least it was tolerable. Rather than blaming herself for being naïve, however, she decides once again to get a couple hours' sleep; she hasn't checked her phone for a while, but as the sun rises, she realizes that it must be almost seven o´clock, and this time she's able to surrender to her fatigue and doesn't wake up until noon.

Immediately after Alicia wakes up, she's thrown right back into her state of shock, checking her phone which lets her know that Johnny is *on my way home, hon.* She hears noise from the children downstairs and, as far as she knows, neither of them has any plans for today. She has already decided that this makes it impossible for her to confront Johnny today. With the four of them in the house, she needs to pretend that everything is alright, but when she gets out of bed, her body tells her how impossible that is going to be, so she goes downstairs to tell the kids that she isn't feeling well and then shortly after returns to her bed. She almost falls asleep again but then detects the sound of Johnny coming home and, knowing that he will be in the bedroom shortly after, pretends to be in a deep sleep; she wants to have the bedroom to herself. She assumes that the kids have told their father that she's sick, and when he enters the bedroom, she soon learns that her plan works; he strokes her cheek and kisses her softly, which makes her scream internally, and then he quietly leaves the bedroom and Alicia stays in there until next morning; the longest and loneliest eighteen hours she has ever spent in her life. She knows that Johnny and the kids will be leaving the house around the same time in the morning and has decided that during breakfast she will let them know that she's still sick, and once everyone has left the house, she will get in the car and go straight to Smith's Carmarket to confront Johnny with her knowledge of his infidelity. A little past 7:30 in the morning, she's alone in the house and has been waiting so many hours to confront Johnny that she wastes no time and finds herself in the car less than ten minutes after that, and upon arriving at his workplace she calls him from the car and asks him to come outside. It takes him a little longer to leave the building than it should, as if he knows that something is up; as if he's trying to buy himself time to come up with an excuse. When she finally sees him in the rearview mirror, he looks like a criminal approaching the witness stand. "Get in," she says loudly as he stands near her door. He rounds the car's hood and gets into the passenger seat, looking at her quizzically.

"I heard you," she states bluntly.

"What do you mean?"

"I heard you on the phone."

"Still not sure what you mean?"

"I heard you having sex." Then she adds more brutally, "No, you were *fucking* her."

"What are you talking about?"

"I'm talking about this weekend. Saturday night, when you called me. Except, you weren't calling. It was a pocket call from your hotel room."

If Johnny had hesitated to leave the building because he was trying to prepare an excuse, he hadn't done a very good job; Alicia's words are followed by sheer silence and the doors of the car seem to be closing in on Johnny. He perspires and looks like a man who would give anything to leave the car, but he knows that doing that is not an option. He also knows that remaining quiet isn't an option, but the otherwise very loquacious man is silenced in a way that he's never been before, and eventually Alicia is the one who breaks the silence.

"I heard it all. I don't know why I sat through it, but I couldn't bring myself to hang up. It felt like forever. As if there was no stopping you."

Johnny's face turns from pale to anemic, and the silence is deafening until he breaks it: "It didn't last very long."

"Is that really what you want to focus on?"

"No, I mean, I just think maybe you got the wrong idea."

"I don't think there's a *right* idea here, is there?" Again, Johnny is speechless for a while, until Alicia continues, "Who is she?"

"Nobody. Honestly, you don't have to worry about who she is. She's nobody."

"Why all the trips to New York then?"

"I've never been with *her* before." Although Johnny is technically telling the truth, there's something about the way he enunciates the word *her*, which instantly makes Alicia analyze the situation differently than she's done so far.

"But you've been with others? Is that it?"

When Johnny doesn't answer Alicia's question right away, she knows that she doesn't need to hear the answer, and the ten-second pause is enough for her. She tells him to get out of the car. He starts mumbling something, but then steps out of the car as she starts pushing him out of it, and, whereas he looked like a criminal approaching the witness stand a few minutes before, he now looks like a criminal who has been convicted of a crime. Through the glass doors of Smith's Carmarket, she sees him talking to his father when she leaves the parking lot, and wonders whether he's telling his father what just happened, or if he will go about his business and pretend that everything is fine. On her way home, she finds herself a bit surprised that he didn't try to deny anything; apparently mentioning the phone call was a smoking gun, and he must have known at once that there was no way he could talk his way out of this.

Once home, Alicia struggles to find peace of mind. She has called in sick and starts to wonder whether that was a bad idea; being alone with her thoughts isn't easy and she considers going for a run but instead ends up walking around in circles in the house. She also considers whether revenge is an option; she has never seen herself as a vindictive person, but now must admit that if she had the chance, she would call Johnny, maybe even facetime him, while she was letting someone take her from behind. It's an ambivalent feeling; while she doesn't like to let her thoughts wander down this path, she's surprised by a simultaneous feeling of arousal. It has been a while since she has felt horny, but the idea of being with another man starts to turn her on and she pauses to think about the fact that she could give in to this desire without feeling bad about it. Anything that can help her is justifiable, and although two wrongs don't make a right, surely her husband couldn't blame her if she copied his behavior.

However, after she's convinced herself that she can easily justify sleeping with someone else than her husband, she soon realizes that even if she wanted to settle the score, she wouldn't know where to begin; she has no "blast from the past" whom she can look up, no neighbor she can start flirting with, nor any colleagues or clients she can seduce. She realizes that she has no go-to guy at all; if she were to act on this, she would have to start from scratch; a Tinder account, a drunken spree somewhere far away from home, or someone from their circle of acquaintances would be her best bet. Right now, none of the above seem obvious to her, and she decides to discard the thought for the time being and instead focus on getting ready for tonight's conversation with Johnny; she has spent the past thirty-two hours reaching the conclusion that this is sufficient grounds for a divorce. Had he cheated on her once, or had it been a spur-of-the-moment thing, it might have been a different story, and she might have been willing to see if she could find it in her heart to forgive him, but the heartless and calculative repetitiveness with which he had planned his adultery makes it impossible for her to imagine continuing her life with him.

She knows that the kids will be home before Johnny, so it's not something they can talk about as soon as she sees him again. Therefore, she decides to go to bed early tonight, as she predicts that he, unlike what he would normally do, will come along because he knows he has to make amends, and then she will tell him there, despite the fact that the bedroom is the last place on earth where she wants to spend time with him.

Chapter three
Gina and Jeremy Smith Vanderbilt

Gina and Jeremy Smith Vanderbilt were conceived in October 2004, in a Park Slope apartment in Brooklyn, when their very drunk father made love to their mother, who was a little less drunk. This was only their thirteenth intercourse, and it wasn't supposed to end in a pregnancy, but the condom burst and they were both so into the act that stopping wasn't an option. It did send the parents-to-be into a state of exhilaration and joyful anticipation but it also opened a Pandora's box of conflicting emotions. Alicia, who had grown up in a home where politics and dinner regularly went hand in hand, was in many ways shaped by the beliefs of her parents, Sharon and James, who were lifelong supporters of the Democratic Party.

Alicia had experienced very few arguments between her parents when they delved into politics, and whenever she did observe a slight difference in opinions between them, she felt comfortable knowing that they would patiently listen to the other's opinion and then peacefully agree to disagree; on the concept of abortion, however, there was nothing they could disagree on, so Alicia knew that telling her parents about her pregnancy wouldn't put them in a dilemma; they would advise her to get an abortion and it would sadden them to know that their daughter had to go through that, but in regard to their political stance there wouldn't be a conflict of interest. In addition to that, their daughter's academic career made the decision even easier; according to them, finishing law school was impossible if you delivered a child into this world, and since they had brought up Alicia in a way that had turned her into an echo of their view on things, they worried little about whether or not she would consider keeping the baby.

Alicia visited Sharon and James three times in the weeks that followed the life-changing and life-creating October night, but failed to mention the pregnancy every time. Each time she regretted it on her way home, and reassured herself that she would do it next time. Knowing that they would encourage her to get an abortion didn't make mentioning the pregnancy easier for her, but she mustered the courage to do it during her fourth post-knowing-I'm-pregnant visit. On this occasion, her parents put on the kids gloves and refrained from mentioning the word abortion. A week later, she invited them to her place and they were also thoughtful enough to not mention it this time, but left her dormroom wondering why she hadn't mentioned anything about her plans, and decided that next time they saw her, they would bring it up if she didn't beat them to it. When they were approaching the end of the next visit, and the apparently unmentionable word had still to be mentioned, James asked a leading question. His exact words were, "But you are going to get an abortion, right?" Alicia's reaction to the question was to burst into tears, and she wasn't able to express herself for a couple of minutes, but eventually was able to confirm that she *was* going to end the pregnancy. She didn't go into anything about being pro-choice, nor did she mention her academic plan. She simply told them that she knew she *had to*, and after her succinct answer Sharon held her for a while, and her father let her know that he was sorry that she had to go through this, and he abstained from letting her know that although he wasn't surprised about her decision, he was still relieved.

On her way home from her parents, Alicia thought about the vast difference that lies in talking about *her* abortion and abortions in general. She remembered how her father had told her the story of how he was there on that January day in 1973, and how he wet the ground outside the Supreme Court with his tears when he realized that Norma McCorvey made history that day. Alicia's father had always wanted to ensure that his daughter knew the main details of what he considered landmark decisions by the Supreme Court; Marbury v. Madison, United States v. Nixon, Brown v. Board of Education. Likewise, he had made it very clear that he considered Roe v. Wade a historical milestone and it was no coincidence that Alicia knew words such as "landmark" and "milestone" before her tenth birthday.

Alicia has also seen a picture of her daughter holding a pro-choice sign, as she rested on her grandfather's shoulder: "Gina and I during a 35th anniversary rally of Roe v. Wade, January 22, 2008", is scribbled in meticulous letters on the back of the polaroid picture. Alicia has often looked at that picture and found it amusing that Gina was but a toddler when her grandfather took her to her first political gathering, and while she has no actual photos to prove it, she has a feeling that she was just as little when her father started dragging her along for similar things. She remembers being thirteen years old when her father filled her in on the details about McCorvey; how this Texan woman was single and unemployed when she became pregnant for the third time, which made her wish for an abortion absolutely fair, according to Alicia's father. He then told Alicia that abortions were illegal in Texas, and that McCorvey became the plaintiff, going by the pseudonym "Jane Roe", who took this case all the way to the Supreme Court and ultimately was the catalyst behind making abortion a "federally protected right"; an expression which you would think a parent would have to clarify for a thirteen-year-old child, but it was unnecessary in this case, as Alicia was already familiar with it.

Likewise, she needed no further explanation of the word "amendment" when her father pointed out that seven of the court's nine justices decided that the 9th and the 14th amendments to the Constitution were "broad enough to encompass a woman's decision whether or not to terminate a pregnancy." For Alicia, thinking about all of this was the easy part; thinking about wanting to utilize her *own* right to an abortion was the difficult part.

After the latest visit, Alicia continued to try to convince herself that terminating the pregnancy was the right thing to do, and that it was something that she shouldn't feel bad about doing, especially since the timing was so obviously off. Meanwhile, she had talked about it with Johnny, who was a Republican, and though he didn't have a die-hard interest in politics, some matters did seem to evoke certain feelings in him, and for as long as he could remember he had been pro-life. He wasn't shaped by his parents' opinion, like Alicia, but, in keeping with the Republican Party policy, he had bought into the idea that preborn children cannot defend their rights, wherefore pro-lifers have to speak for them, and despite not being particularly religious he did believe that a life is granted inherent value by the God who creates it in its mother's womb. Consequently, Johnny was against it when Alicia told him that she planned on having an abortion.

It had taken a couple of weeks for her to muster the courage to let him know that she was pregnant, whereafter it took another two weeks to find the courage to tell him that she was planning on having an abortion. At the time, politics wasn't something they spent much time discussing, but coincidentally they had talked about abortion, and while it hadn't been a major issue, one of the things that did make it difficult for Alicia to tell Johnny about the pregnancy was knowing that she was pro-choice and he was pro-life.

As it turned out, however, the conversation was never a heated one; Johnny didn't hesitate to remind her that he was against abortions, and he would prefer that *their* child was brought into this world, but he also had to admit that he hadn't imagined becoming a parent in his early twenties, and his attempt to change her mind was rather half-hearted. Little by little, he also seemed to change his mind, and less than a week after she had told him about her plans, he told her that he had regretted his reaction; he'd had a change of heart and was now one hundred percent behind her and her decision and declared that she should get it done as soon as possible. Essentially, the situation didn't look overwhelmingly complicated for Alicia; she had decided not to go through with the pregnancy, she knew it was the right thing to do, and both her parents and her boyfriend supported her in this, so she went to DeKalb Avenue and scheduled an appointment in one of the local abortion clinics. The procedure was to be done three weeks after she reached out to them, and then after a couple of days of rest she could resume to her normal YLS life and focus on legal research, theory, writing, and analysis, moot court competitions, law journals, guidance from faculty advisors, career development plans, and summer internships, rather than breast changes, implantation bleeding, frequent urination, bloating, constipation, and overwhelming fatigue.

To this day, Gina and Jeremy Smith Vanderbilt don't know anything about the fact that their lives came close to never happening. They've talked about the concept of abortion with their parents, but it has been a political or ideological discussion; something that involved the lives of *others*. They know nothing about how their mother had initially planned to end the pregnancy, in accordance with their father's and their grandparents' wishes. Likewise, they don't know anything about why their mother changed her mind. It wasn't a sudden change of heart; until Alicia was six weeks into her pregnancy, she was certain that she wasn't destined to be the mother of the fetuses that she was carrying. It wasn't any fetal movement, as it was too early for this, that started to change Alicia's mind; instead, she found herself going to bed one night thinking, what if this is the only time that I will ever become pregnant, will I then regret this decision for the rest of my life? The next morning the thought was gone, and she spent a good two or three days without any cold feet until one night, when the thought entered her mind again right before bedtime. This time, the notion didn't evaporate, and she spent the following days rethinking everything she had ever thought about abortions; she continued to believe that abortions were not wrong, but just as the babies were growing inside her uterus, a new sentiment had grown inside her mind; abortions were wrong *for her*.

By now, all this thinking had made Alicia so lightheaded that she didn't know what to expect from Johnny when she told him that she had changed her mind and intended to keep the baby–she didn't know at the time that it was a two-package deal. She was also too exhausted to worry about his reaction and therefore took little notice of the fact that he did object a bit to her change of heart. According to him, they had an agreement, and, moreover, he didn't think that she could decide this without having discussed it with him.

Obviously, this wasn't the reaction Alicia had hoped for, but she soon found comfort in the fact that his objections were, after all, quite short-lived; first of all, it was difficult for a pro-life guy to object to the fact that his girlfriend didn't want an abortion. Secondly, he, unlike her, didn't have to worry about any changes in his career plans as he didn't have any. He knew that he wasn't planning on bartending for the rest of his life, but that was about the extent of his aspirations; he had no idea where he would be five or ten years down the road, so the baby couldn't disrupt anything in his life, and the truth of the matter was that although he continued to think that they were too young for kids, he also slowly started to feel something akin to excitement and pride when he contemplated the idea that he was going to be somebody's father in a not-so-distant future.

While the situation had now become somewhat paradoxical, a Democrat who was for abortions ended up not wanting one, and a Republican who was against abortions ended up reprobating the fact that his girlfriend wasn't going to get one, and while the whole baby-or-not baby-thing did leave them both with a feeling that maybe they didn't see eye to eye as much as they had imagined, the pregnancy came and went without any major arguments. Johnny lived up to his responsibility and supported Alicia through morning sickness, constipation, and her ever-growing fatigue.

It was a minor shock when they learned that there wasn't just *one* baby on its way; at twenty-one, it seemed overwhelming that the sole responsibility of *a* completely innocent and helpless *baby*–not plural– would soon be placed upon their shoulders, especially since neither of them had much experience with children, let alone infants who couldn't even hold their heads up.

As such, the thought of *two* babies sapped their strength entirely. They had already decided that the Park Slope apartment was large enough for their little family addition, but now they had to reconsider whether it was large enough for twins. As if these speculations weren't stressful enough in themselves, it added pressure to Alicia that she had to consider these things while her body was undergoing major changes; weight gain in a twin pregnancy exceeds weight gain in a single-fetus pregnancy because of greater increases in both maternal tissues and intrauterine weight, and she wasn't many months into her pregnancy before getting out of bed in the morning was enervating, and in the final stretch of her pregnancy simple things such as brushing her teeth or making a sandwich ran her ragged. Still, the time when Alicia carried the babies inside her were, in most ways, good months, and the birth of them marked the beginning of what were probably the best years of her relationship with Johnny.

Johnny supported Alicia as best as he could during the pregnancy, but he did it because he had to and because it was the right thing to do. He felt only somewhat connected to the baby, and he didn't feel that it was bringing them closer together; technically, it was *their* baby, but it was *her* pregnancy. When he was with friends or family he spoke little of the baby and gave casual answers when asked about it; at times, he almost seemed to forget about its existence. Since Alicia hadn't permanently moved in with him yet, he wasn't constantly reminded of the life-changing event that awaited him and, on days when they didn't speak on the phone, he would go about his business as if his life was the same as it had always been. He went out a lot and, on some nights, he drank excessively because he wanted to enjoy the waning months of freedom to the fullest. He knew the deadline for this hedonistic lifestyle; they had agreed that Alicia would move in with him in May and when the babies were born, in July 2005, Johnny knew that his days of hitting the town were, at least for a while, brought to an end.

Somewhat to his surprise, however, being a parent rather than a partygoer was very easy for him; he held those infants for the first time, first Gina, then Jeremy, and he felt their tiny fingers and looked at their eyes, which he instinctively knew were beautiful, despite them being closed, and then he surrendered to the exhilaration of the moment; the babies were no longer some abstract, in-utero beings whose heartbeat, skin, hair, and bodies were shielded from him. It's sometimes said that a woman becomes a mother the day she becomes pregnant, while a man becomes a father the day his child is born, and this statement was in many ways true for Johnny; the second Gina and Jeremy went ex-utero, they were *his* babies as well, and the realization that those little beings were now a part of his life forever left Johnny in tears of joy. Soon after their birth, he got to lie down with the babies and felt the warmth of their little bodies against his chest in a moment of pivotal skin-to-skin contact. There was almost a third birth of the day; at this moment, Johnny was no longer a party animal who was barely out of his teenage years; he was born as a man on the same day that his children were born, and, at least for some time, he was a man who was mature beyond his years.

Alicia was equally overjoyed when she went from being a pregnant woman to a new mother. She soon felt relieved that the pregnancy was finally over and looked forward to getting to know the babies that had caused her body so much distress. Also, she couldn't wait to bring her body back to its pre-pregnant state. Her postpartum period was predominantly happy, despite the seemingly unavoidable lapses into the baby blues, and although she was a young mother, it took her less than a year to feel that she was an experienced mother. Unlike Johnny, she didn't need to become a parent to mature, but the birth of her children still changed her in a significant way; she began to realize that there was more to life than grades, papers, projects, and presentations–if it was meant to be, she would pass the bar someday, but if it wasn't, she would find something else to do. A mature-enough realization in itself, though her parents didn't necessarily see it like that.

For the first time in her life, she decided to let the chips fall where they may, a sentiment which offered her a feeling of serenity which was not only healthy for her, but also for her relationship.

Alicia decided that she wanted to be a stay-at-home mom until the twins were at least three years old. She had saved up a substantial amount of money and no longer needed to worry about expenses for university fees, housing, and books. Ever since she was a teenager, her parents had told her that they would support her through law school, so although it was a disappointment to them that she quit her studies, they decided that some of the "Yale money" was now "baby money". Her mother wanted to give Alicia a thousand dollars per month and her father wanted to give her five hundred dollars per month, and since her father was the wealthier of the two, and the cheapest one, a compromise was made which provided Alicia with six hundred and seventy-five dollars per month for her living expenses until July 2008, which should make it possible to make ends meet for three years; a decent amount of time for Alicia to figure out what she wanted to do with her life, once the babies were no longer babies.

The money she received from her parents, a sum of saved-up money, and the money that Johnny made bartending was enough for them to make a decent living as a family. Once all expenses were taken care of, there was usually a spare amount which also made it possible for them to occasionally take the kids to a restaurant, a children's museum, or even an amusement park. However, Alicia and Johnny soon realized that babies and toddlers were easily amused; the local park was just as good as any amusement park and eating in was just as good as eating out, so once the twins had celebrated their first birthday, they decided to put a little cash aside to be ready if they one day decided to leave the city. At the time, moving to a suburb was something they had only briefly talked about, but it was inevitable that they both started to come to the realization that extra square feet and a fenced garden came with a number of advantages. It was not that they didn't enjoy raising kids in the city; there were plenty of parks and playgrounds, there were other kids in the neighborhood, and whenever one of them wanted a break from the twins, any form of entertainment or distraction was right outside their front door.

The first thirty-six months of the babies' lives was a time during which Johnny and Alicia felt a connection that they hadn't shared before and wouldn't share after. Naturally, raising twins was the most strenuous thing either one of them had ever tried; they lived through the constant changing of diapers, the continuous nap routines, and the incessant task of cleaning up food that was everywhere except in the mouths of the children. In addition to that, there were the ceaseless nights when at least one of the twins, and sometimes both of them, kept them awake, not to mention the persistent tantrums which started when the twins were approximately two years old. Sometimes either Alicia or Johnny had to take a walk in the park, because their life was no walk in the park, but the happy moments outweighed all the frustrations and there was never a moment of regret for either of the parents. Any and all thoughts about abortion evaporated the moment the babies opened their eyes.

Even Alicia's father, who had been against the idea of his daughter becoming a mother at twenty-one, making him a grandfather at forty-nine, embraced the babies to the point where it was obvious that being a granddad was now a part of who he was and plenty were the days and weekends when he and his wife made sure to see their grandchildren, so as to reduce the risk of missing out on their first words or steps or any other significant aspect of a child's development. Never once did James mention that having the babies was a bad idea and it was as if he simply lost his interest in the entire issue of abortion. The once devoted pro-choicer stopped paying attention to the abortion debate and for several years you would have thought that the word had disappeared from his vocabulary because he so rarely engaged in conversations about it.

In June 2022, however, James couldn't steer clear of debate any longer, when the Supreme Court overturned Roe v. Wade and the constitutional right to abortion that had been the law nationwide for almost fifty years. He was outraged for a long time, and a year later, for the first time in several years, he took to the streets, on the day that could have been the fiftieth anniversary of Roe v. Wade, and joined those protestors in support of abortion rights who desired to promote their idea of what a post-Roe America should be like. James cursed Donald Trump, which he often did, and execrated Neil Gorsuch, Brett Kavanaugh, and Amy Coney Barrett, whom Alicia's father, prior to 2022, had rarely given any thought to, but now held in contempt for blindly following the ideas of the man who had appointed them. Objectively, he should have been filled with just as much disdain for Samuel Alito and Clarence Thomas, who were the two other justices who secured the 5-4 Supreme Court decision that overturned Roe v. Wade, but there was something about those three other justices that made them the worst; it was likely the fact that he merely regarded them as extensions of Trump's power.

In the months after the reversal of Roe v. Wade, James grew exceedingly frustrated as he watched more and more states ceasing nearly all abortion care, and his anger culminated in January 2024 when he turned on the TV and happened to overhear Trump's (in)famous remarks during a Fox News town hall in Des Moines: "For fifty-four years they were trying to get Roe v. Wade terminated, and I did it, and I'm proud to have done it. Nobody else was going to get that done but me, and we did it, and we did something that was a miracle."

Alicia's father felt an almost uncontrollable urge to throw things at the TV when he heard this, and comments like this made him worry about what this country was turning into. Although Trump did offer some nuances, and despite his history of switching between pro-choice and pro-life, James only heard those three words:

"I did it", which was probably a natural reaction for any Democrat and, shortly after the interview, Joe Biden's X account released a video clip in which they commented on Trump's answer: "Just like he said: he did it." For Alicia's father, this confirmed his conviction that Trump was first and foremost pro-life, and any attempts to add nuances to this were electoral expediency; just another one of his attempts to walk the fine line between satisfying his conservative base while at the same time not scaring off too many potential voters.

The overturning of Roe v. Wade had the same impact on Alicia, though not to the same extent as her father. She discussed the situation with her parents, which was a reminder of how she had once been a woman who had considered an abortion. However, this train of thought immediately gave way to the assurance that delivering Gina and Jeremy into this world had been the right decision. Alicia remembers how, after two years of baby-bliss in New York, she and Johnny entered a more dedicated phase of house-hunting and their first decision was agreeing upon the fact that only four states could be considered: Connecticut, Massachusetts, Vermont, and New York. Shortly after that, they agreed upon two things. One was that the right house was more important than the right state, and the other was that they wouldn't mind living close to their own or the other's parents, so when the perfect house was put up for sale in Cold Spring they opted for it, and in the summer of 2008 the twins were sent to Alicia's parents' place for a long weekend while Alicia and Johnny spent a couple of days packing all their belongings in the Park Slope apartment and then a couple of days unpacking them in the house in Cold Spring. When Alicia's parents brought the kids to their new home, Johnny and Alicia felt certain that the day marked the beginning of a new and gleeful chapter in their lives.

Chapter four
Barack Hussain Obama II

It's the morning after Alicia has told Johnny that she intends to file for a divorce, and both have, without planning it, called in sick. Had Alicia known that Johnny would call in sick, she might have gone to work, as they are, with the kids having gone to school, now left all by themselves in a house that appears to be more silent than ever before. They do say good morning to each other and ask the other if they have slept okay, but that is far as the communication goes. Normally, after waking up, you slowly start to speak more and more; today, both of them become increasingly stifled as the morning proceeds.

The kids have forgotten to turn off the TV, so their silence is interrupted by the story of how Joe Biden, supported by Obama and Clinton, hauled in a record twenty-six million dollars for his reelection campaign at a fundraiser at Radio City Music Hall in New York. Under normal circumstances they would dwell on this, and it might lead to some sort of argument between them; Johnny would go on about how he could *tolerate* Clinton, but he wouldn't miss out on the opportunity of complaining about how he's sick and tired of Obama meddling in everything and he might repeat his standard phrase about him: "I disapproved of him before he became president, I detested him while he was president, and I still despise him after his presidency." Alicia would be provoked by this, despite having heard it countless times over the years, and she would defend

Obama and mention the Affordable Care Act, the repeal of the Don't Ask, Don't Tell policy, the Deferred Action for Childhood Arrivals, and the Paris Agreement, respectively Obama's top one, two, three, and four accomplishments, according to her. Mentioning this was Alicia's way of letting Johnny know that no other president could ever have achieved such fine accomplishments. Johnny would object to this and repeat what he had repeated on so many other occasions, namely that the killing of Osama Bin Laden is the only Obama-achievement worth mentioning, whereupon they would bicker over this for a while.

Paradoxically enough, however, they are on such bad terms now that they cannot even argue about things. Arguing, for Alicia, would mean engaging in a conversation with Johnny, and she prefers to avoid this, and Johnny simply doesn't know what to say; he lacks a verbal knife to cut the silence. Not even the joke made by the moderator—that the three presidents had come to town, but not one of them to appear in court—brings out a reaction from either of them. They could have used it to discuss whether Trump's legal troubles should be seen as a witch hunt or as completely fair reactions to his transgressions. He would argue in favor of the former, and she would argue in favor of the latter, and the room would be filled with dissension, but at least it would be filled with something. On a good day, they might even have avoided the argument and just grinned at it, acknowledging the fact that the moderator's comment was, despite their personal views, a good one. Today, there are no grins and no arguing, and it becomes increasingly obvious to them that the only thing worse than arguing, in a situation like this, is *not* arguing, as the deafening silence is more corrosive than a heated discussion. Ultimately, this is also what leads Johnny to break the silence.

"Honey, isn't there anything we can do to talk about this? How about I just move out for a few days, and then you have some time to think it through?"

"First of all, don't *honey* me. I'm not your honey anymore and never will be again. And I *did* think it through. Thinking even more about it isn't going to change my mind. Tomorrow, the day after tomorrow, next week, month or year, I'll still feel the same way; I cannot live with you anymore. You can move out for a few days, sure. Then I can tell the kids, and we can both get ready to sort out all the details."

"The kids, exactly. It would be so much better if we didn't have to tell them this. We should give it a try at least, for their sakes."

Although his argument in itself is valid, it infuriates Alicia that *he's* the one who mentions their children; they become hostages in his argumentation, she thinks, and discards the idea immediately: "What would have been better for our kids would've been growing up with a father who can keep his dick in his pants when he leaves town. So, don't you tell me what's best for our kids."

"Okay, well, I didn't mean it like that. It's for *our* sakes that we should try to get through this. I don't think one mistake is enough to throw all of this away. We have so much going for us."

"*One* mistake?"

"You know what I mean."

"No, I don't know what you mean. *One* time would have been a mistake; several times is a pattern."

"But I can change; I know, I can."

"You don't know anything. And even if you did, I don't; that's the problem."

Their talk is followed by another few minutes of silence, whereupon Alicia turns her back to him and says that she needs to be alone for a while. Either he leaves the house for the rest of the day or she does, Alicia clarifies, and since he acknowledges that it would be inappropriate not to go along with her wishes, Johnny gets ready to leave the house. Despite not knowing what to say, he tries to initiate a conversation once again, but his inability to express himself makes it very easy for Alicia not to turn around, so she continues to stare out the window as he leaves the house.

Even after she hears the door shutting behind him, her eyes remain fixated for a while; she's overlooking their patio and garden and questioning whether Johnny had a point in saying that they have so much going for them. At this exact time of the day, on the exact outdoor furniture that she's staring at right now, they've shared countless cups of coffee over the years, and plenty of afternoons watching their children play in the garden, followed by a barbecue, which brought them together as one, small, happy family. Although the kids are more-or-less grown up by now and the family gatherings don't happen as frequently anymore, divorcing Johnny means they will never happen again; the family barbeques will be over, and so will Christmas, Thanksgiving, Easter, birthdays, Mother's Day and Father's Day dinners, and all other occasions that traditionally gather the four of them around their table. Likewise, they will never again shove the kids into the car and head on out to explore the American homeland. A few years ago, they went on a west coast road trip which took them to all the unmissable spots between San Diego and Del Norte, and it was such a good experience that they never stopped talking about wanting to do a similar trip on their *own* coast. They were past the days when the kids became impatient in a car, and they had seriously considered going all the way down to Key West whenever the timing was right.

Now, the timing would never be right. Sure, she could do all these things with the kids by herself, but doing it as a family would never be an option again, and maybe Johnny was right when he said that throwing all that away was too much. Was the punishment worse than the crime? Was he right in saying that he could change and was she wrong in thinking that it would be impossible to forgive him? She could never get any guarantees that he wouldn't do the same thing to her again; it would be a leap she would have to take—but could she rule out the possibility that she could do just that? With no one to talk to about all of this, tears again become the silent language of Alicia's heart and she forces herself out of the apathy by going out on the patio which she has been staring at for the past hour. Once there, the fresh air slowly turns her into a more self-composed version of herself, and she reminds herself that she has more reasons to divorce Johnny than to forgive him. Johnny's infidelity cannot be reduced to the straw that broke the camel's back; while the unfaithfulness was the worst thing and ultimately the catalyst behind the divorce, it's also clear to her that their problems started long before her husband put his dick into strange women.

Alicia doesn't shut the patio door when she goes outside, and the news from the TV is looping, so she once again hears the Biden/Obama/Clinton fundraiser story, and her thoughts take her back to Obama's time; a somewhat happy time, she remembers, because they settled into their new home, but she also identifies it as the time when their matrimonial conflicts started. Prior to 2008, they didn't dwell an awful lot on politics, as they, little by little, had come to realize how much they disagreed upon, but it hadn't been a problem for them. Johnny liked George Bush Jr, she didn't; not necessarily the end of story, but not the beginning of an argument either.

It was a different story with Barach Hussain Obama II. Alicia and Johnny's problems went beyond political dissent, but Obama became the catalyst that in many ways slowly changed their perception of their spouse; it didn't begin when he became the forty-fourth leader of the free world; it started when he, once and for all, entered the nationwide, political stage and delivered his first keynote address. In a state of grief and sorrow, accompanied by a glass of whiskey, Alicia Clare Vanderbilt finds herself thinking back to that July night twenty years ago when the Illinois senator stepped onto the stage at the Democratic National Convention and delivered a vision for the country that elected him as the first Black president four later. She still remembers the exact words: "There's not a liberal America and a conservative America. There's the United States of America. There's not a Black America and white America and Latino America and Asian America; there's the United States of America." These words, to Alicia's ears, were so shrouded in compassion and hope, and so elegantly delivered, that she started to believe that this young senator was somehow right. His sheer enunciation of the word "united" made her believe that her country was just that.

She sat through the entirety of the speech and when she talked about it with friends, family, and fellow students, and even some of her teachers, she sensed that they were all on the same page; this was probably the best keynote address ever. It was so optimistic and was presented with such charisma that the listeners were left with the idea that the man behind the words was a man of more than just words; in so far as it can be said that Obama's road to the White House began that night, there's no doubt that Alicia, and millions of Americans across the country, went to bed thinking that there he was; the man who could change this country for the better.

A few days after Obama's oration, Alicia went to New York to visit Johnny. She hadn't planned beforehand that she wanted to talk about Obama with him, and they didn't, until the day after she went there, when the subject just came up during their morning coffee. She didn't expect him to appreciate the finer semantic details of the speech, such as the incorporation of the Latin term *E pluribus unum*; "out of many, one", nor did she expect him to fully embrace the concluding words, "out of this long political darkness, a brighter day will come." However, she did expect him to appreciate that a politician wanted the United States of America to be *united.* No one, in her opinion, could have anything against a sentiment like that, and while Johnny didn't specifically voice his disagreement, he did mumble something about the problems with Blacks and Latinos. He was doing other stuff and roaming the apartment during their conversation, wherefore it could hardly be called a conversation, and ultimately, Alicia was merely left with the *impression* that Johnny disliked Blacks and Latinos, and that he didn't share the belief that Barack Hussain Obama II or John Kerry, whom Obama supported at the time, would ever be the right president for the US. She couldn't point to anything specific that he had said, nor did he come across as a sheer racist, but there was something in his reaction to her mentioning Obama that had rubbed her the wrong way.

However, it was a beautiful New York weekend and she was in the process of falling in love with this guy, and maybe it would be better to give him the benefit of the doubt; maybe he didn't mean what he had said—actually, he had hardly said anything—and it was for the better not to dwell on this. Going too deep into his reaction could be a waste of a good day, and they only had a few hours left before she had to return to Yale, so they carried on with their day and their lives, and paid no particular attention to this upcoming political superstar from Illinois. In the weeks and months that followed, they hardly ever spoke about him, and then, suddenly, a year later, she was pregnant and nine months after that the twins were born, marking the beginning of a period which provided even less time to focus on, let alone argue over, political matters.

This no-talk-of-politics period was never something they explicitly agreed to go through, but it was inevitable that they both enjoyed it; watching the baby twins babbling, cooing, smiling, blowing bobbles, exploring their own feet, and reaching out for Alicia and Johnny was just more life-affirming than delving into the great recession, the unemployment rate, the wars in Iraq and Afghanistan, the energy prices, and environmental concerns. Perhaps they both subconsciously knew that not getting too much into the state of affairs of the nation was a way of steering clear of arguments and instead focusing on becoming a family, and it was in many ways the most wholesome period of their marriage.

However, Johnny and Alicia knew that this grace period wouldn't last forever and when the calendar said 2008, talking about the upcoming presidential election was virtually unavoidable. In so far as they could limit the time that *they* spent talking about the election, it was impossible for them to put a limit on everyone else; their friends and families spoke about it at length and even strangers in stores, playgrounds, trains, restaurants or wherever they went were inclined to initiate conversations about the exciting race between the young, upcoming, charismatic, Black superstar and the old, conservative war hero. It didn't come as a surprise to Alicia that Johnny supported John McCain. It wasn't only John McCain's political vision, it was also his valor that made Johnny respect him so much; his military service, his years as a prisoner of war during which he endured torture that left him with lasting physical disabilities, and his medals and commendations made him the all-American, obvious choice as president, according to Johnny. Alicia admired Obama for his intellect, his rhetoric skills, the vision that he mapped out for the American people, and the magna cum laude graduation from Harvard Law School. It was a bit simpler with Johnny, who admired McCain for his stoicism; the Flying Cross and the Purple Heart were testaments to McCain's gallantry, just as the Silver Star and the Bronze Star proved that he, not the other candidate, was the star.

Fortunately for Johnny, a lot of people agreed with him, but unfortunately for him, more people agreed with Alicia, and so the result of the 2008 election didn't come as a surprise; the economic crisis, the public desire for change, Obama's charismatic campaign, and the Democratic momentum from the 2006 midterm elections all contributed to a fairly predictable victory for Barack Obama, and Alicia quickly learned that Johnny was a bit more vocal in his reaction than had been the case a few years before, when she had praised Obama so much for his keynote address. He wasn't mumbling this time and there was no room for misinterpretation in his reaction; Obama as senator was one thing—Obama as president was something else entirely. Johnny was exceedingly upset about the election; so much that he spent November 6th alone, because he needed to "clear his mind". His frustrations were mainly expressed through political language; he thought that Obama was much too progressive and radical on issues such as healthcare reform, taxation, and government spending;

he thought that Obama would be incapable of handling the economic recovery; he thought that merely a few years of experience as a senator was hardly enough to prepare him for the complexities of the presidency. And, when Johnny ran out of arguments, which he sometimes did, he resorted to more plain comments about Obama; "There's just something about him that I don't like," and Alicia decided not to ask him to elaborate on what that *something* was.

The closest he came to defining what something about him meant was stating how ridiculous he considered the whole *Obama-is-the-personification-of-Martin-Luther-King-Jr.'s-dream narrative.*

Martin Luther King Jr. was at least fighting for a reasonable cause, according to Johnny, but he continuously stressed that the fight was over; it no longer made sense to discuss racial inequality, simply because there was none of it.

To the best of Johnny's belief, whatever grievances and challenges African Americans faced were self-inflicted rather than systemic; a Black man had all the same opportunities in the US as a white man, and he considered it harmful that a Black man was now telling the Black population that they didn't get their share.

The following eight years only served to aggravate Johnny even more as he believed that he now witnessed a president who was fighting a fight that didn't need to be fought. The Fair Sentencing Act, the Clemency Initiative, the My Brother's Keeper Initiative, the Pell Grants, and the Affirmatively Furthering Fair Housing Rule passed by Obama were bound to catalyze two things. First, Johnny's blood pressure went up and secondly, once again the differences between Alicia and Johnny were made increasingly visible; she always considered these Obama achievements sensible and necessary, and he always thought the opposite, and maybe it was in the back of their minds that whenever they were discussing the growing polarization in American politics, they were really just describing themselves.

During these years, Johnny also underwent the transformation that is now catapulting his life in an entirely new direction; the otherwise faithful man, who had matured so much after the birth of his children, cheated on his wife for the first time, and since he so quickly developed a taste for the forbidden fruit, it was just a matter of time before he did it again. And again. And again. And, before Johnny knew it, he was addicted to his secret lifestyle and started thinking that since he had already cheated on Alicia a handful of times, it wouldn't make a difference if he did it again. And again, and again, and again.

Eight years come and go fast when you are busy raising kids, and as Obama's presidency was coming to an end, Johnny started to feel a surge of relief. He had bought into the idea that once Obama stepped down, it would be possible to "Make America great again". Even Obama's very last actions couldn't squander Johnny's optimism. The soon-ex-president granted clemency to 330 individuals on his last full day in office, which meant that he, during his entire presidency, granted clemency to a total of 1,927 individuals; a record high number. This could have left Johnny with a bitter taste in his mouth; he could have dwelled on how this showed that Obama was soft and he could have convinced himself that most of the 1,927 individuals were probably Blacks who didn't deserve either a commutation or a pardon, but he didn't worry too much about it because he was certain that Trump would clean up this mess.

Simultaneously, he could have asked Alicia whether she didn't agree that granting clemency to 330 individuals in *one* day wasn't stretching it a bit; it was such a staggering number of people; enough to make up an entire village and surely she could also see that this was, at least to some extent, virtue signaling. And he came close to bringing it up, but was scrolling his Facebook-page and stumbled upon a post which expressed an opinion similar to his own: *Wonder how many Black criminals Obama put back on the streets today?* He didn't know the guy behind the post, but he took to reading a number of the comments and then, just as he was about to put the phone down, he noticed his wife's comment:

Obama's clemency decisions are driven by a broader agenda to address issues within the criminal justice system, particularly the disparities and harsh sentences associated with non-violent drug offenses. While a significant number of those who received clemency were African Americans, this reflects the racial disparities present in the U.S. criminal justice system rather than a specific favoritism based on race. Many individuals serving disproportionately long sentences for drug offenses are African American due to the systemic biases and policies, such as mandatory minimum sentences and the crack cocaine sentencing disparity, that disproportionately affect Black communities.

Obama's clemency efforts aim to rectify some of these injustices and are part of a larger movement towards criminal justice reform. Thus, while a notable number of African Americans benefit from Obama's clemency actions, this is more an outcome of addressing systemic issues rather than a focus on race.

Disproportionately my ass! Johnny thought and as soon as he was done reading the last line, he discarded the idea of addressing the issue with her. This was so progressive, so woke, so *her*—nothing good would come from mentioning that he shared the opinion of the man behind the post rather than her opinion. Besides, Obama was almost yesterday's news; a new president would be inaugurated the day after

It's almost noon now, and Alicia is done with her whiskey (both a first and a second glass) and she has stopped questioning whether divorcing Johnny is the right decision. She has spent the last couple of hours since he left the house by thinking about how different they are, accentuated by differing views on ex-presidents, and she knows that any time spent dwelling on Obama's successor is bound to reinforce the impression that they're a couple who have grown increasingly unaligned over time.

Moreover, the phone call from the other night is haunting her mind again; the sensual sounds, from both her husband and the woman, keep popping up in her head; silently and ephemerally to begin with, but then they gain force and become consistent to the point where she ends up shaking her head, hoping that will make the sounds disappear. When that doesn't work, she decides two things. First of all, she makes a deal with herself never to question whether a divorce is the right thing, and secondly, she enters the house and pours herself a third whiskey.

Chapter five
Donald John Trump

Unlike the election of Obama in 2008, and the one four years later, which were both fairly predictable, the 2016 election surprised both Americans and observers outside America. The Republican nominee had no political experience, his campaign was poorly organized, and he became herostratically famous for nicknaming political opponents: Lyin' Ted, Low-Energy Jeb, Little Marco, Sloppy Steve, Sneaky Dianne, and Crooked Hillary were but some of the politicians who suddenly found their names paired with a less flattering adjective. Johnny found most of these nicknames funny and had a particular penchant for Crooked Hillary; he, like many other Republicans, considered the nickname extraordinarily fitting.

No one embodied the establishment more than her. She was too elitist, too out of sync with the average American, too alien for someone like him, he figured, and relished the idea that Trump made such a huge deal out of Clinton's use of a private email server, set up in her home, for not only personal but also official communication. This was just what Trump needed; her not using the official State Department email system was proof that there was something putrescent about her, and his incessant questioning of her judgement and trustworthiness was, according to Johnny, a perfect backdrop for the entire election cycle; he, too, started to adopt the idea that Clinton was just as crooked as Trump claimed, and he embraced the nickname to the point that he almost forgot what her real surname was. Occasionally, Johnny made sure to point out that his critique of her was not gender-based; he didn't agree with those who believed that the nation wasn't ready for a female president; he just didn't believe that it was ready for *her*. Insofar as Johnny supported Trump, him being satisfied with the 2016 election was just as much a testament to his disapproval of Hillary Clinton as it was an appraisal of Donald Trump and on November 8, 2016, he went to bed thinking that the result was like two victories in one night; her defeat was just as much a victory as his triumph.

Johnny liked almost everything about Donald Trump, but there were a few things about him that rubbed him the wrong way; Trump's "I like people who don't get caught" comment about John McCain was one of them. This was no way to talk about a war hero, Johnny thought. Yet things like that were details and at the end of the day, he bought into the narrative. The MAGA slogan worked with Johnny, and the day after the election he felt like celebrating, but the kids were too young to really understand what was going on, let alone talk about it, and, though he knew his odds were low, he asked Alicia if she wanted to have a couple of drinks with him after the kids were tucked in. She diplomatically declined by letting him know that she had a headache and really needed a good night's sleep. He asked her again the day after, and even asked her three days after the election as well, but her reply was the same every night. In fact, on the third night, her headache had gotten worse, maybe because she wasn't sleeping well those days. After that, he stopped asking for a long time.

Four days after the election, Johnny went to a bar after work, and on his way home he decided that as soon as he saw Alicia, he would ask her what she really thought about Trump. He knew how touchy it was, and realized that it might lead to some kind of argument. Essentially, he wanted to test whether they were able to have a conversation about Trump. They had talked a great deal about him, but surely there was a difference between her view on Trump, the candidate, and Trump, the president.

Her reaction to him opening up this talk was that she didn't know where to start. Initially, she said something about how she resented the "grab 'em by the pussy" comment, and he had to give it to her; he didn't like that either. Following this, she said something about the US-Mexico wall and how she was sick of hearing the phrase "build that wall". She mentioned the date June 16, 2015, which was the day Johnny and Alicia were at her parents' place and listened to Trump's announcement speech, during which he outlined his opinion on immigration and border security, and with fierce eyes declared the need for a physical barrier on the US-Mexico border. The twins were playing in the garden, Alicia was reading *The New York Times*, her parents were getting ready to prepare dinner, and Johnny was napping on the couch, when Trump appeared on the screen and quickly managed to catch the attention of everyone in the house.

While it was in every possible way a perfectly normal day, they soon realized that what they were watching on TV was out of the ordinary; this was a businessman turned celebrity, whose communication style was so direct and unfiltered that it was impossible for them to know what to make of him as a politician. Although Johnny was the least knowledgeable of the four when it came to politics, he sensed something that the others didn't quite sense that night; Trump's way of addressing immigration could take him all the way to the White House. He didn't use the exact phrase "build that wall" during his announcement speech, but it was obvious to everyone that constructing a border wall was a pivotal component of his policy.

From time to time, Johnny took his eyes off the screen and looked at his wife and his parents-in-law instead; he sensed a sort of fear in their eyes, but more so than that he sensed a sort of arrogance. After listening to the speech for ten minutes, he anticipated that Alicia's father would soon turn off the TV and Johnny's intuition proved right; James turned off the TV before the speech was over and emphasized that there was "no need to give Trump the time of day."

Following this, he assumed the role of the protective, know-it-all father figure who provides solace for his wife and daughters. His exact words were: "He's not gonna get elected anyway, so there's no need to waste time listening to him." It was uncertain to Johnny whether the words were also aimed at him; however, it was certain that he didn't agree with them.

In the weeks and months that followed, the idea of building a wall turned into a specific chant, which became a rallying cry among Trump supporters. The phrase was so succinct and memorable that Trumpsters could not but shout it in unison at the megalomaniac rallies, which were yet another unusual way of campaigning. Those three words slowly became a key part of the political discourse surrounding Trump's candidacy, and while Johnny himself never made his way to a Trump rally, plenty were the occasions where he watched and enjoyed how thousands of people chanted "Build that wall"; every time he witnessed that on TV, he had a beer. And whenever the chant was followed by another one: "Lock her up," he had two beers. It became his own discrete way of looking forward to the day, when Trump would begin to "drain the swamp."

During the course of 2016, Johnny felt more and more confident that Trump would defeat Clinton; it was obvious to him that "Build that wall" was not just a powerful slogan in itself, but was also a part of a broader, equally powerful message: "Make America Great Again". Trump's ability to use social media, and generally to dominate media coverage, made sure that his promise to bring jobs back to the US reached out to, and struck a chord with, millions of voters. Trump came across as a newcomer and assumed that position to perfection. He tapped into a similar feeling that grew in Johnny, when he was watching the announcement speech surrounded by people who were far more educated than himself: his father-in-law was a compliance officer and his mother-in-law was a political science professor, and his wife, who had been stripped of the opportunity of achieving a similarly prestigious education because of the birth of their twins, had still somehow ended up far closer to the establishment than himself.

The three of them didn't just read *The New York Times*; they had it written all over them. Johnny had never really felt that Obama appealed to him, but he considered Hillary Clinton even more alienated from the general population. Her words resonated among people like his parents-in-law and his wife, Trump's words resonated with guys like him; Trump was an outsider who spoke to other outsiders and assured them that the US was not just for the distinctly literate, highly-educated, upper-class urbanites; it was also for guys, AMERICAN guys, who made a living selling used cars in their father's auto shop.

Johnny was certain that Trump would be his voice, and when he spoke of his famous wall, Johnny didn't think about the fact that whenever he spoke about this bulwark with Alicia and her parents, they weren't just talking about the physical barrier that Trump hoped to build on the US-Mexico border; they were also indirectly talking about the wall that was starting to build between people *like them* and guys *like him* and perhaps they were also speaking of an already existing wall between his wife and him which continued to grow larger.

Alicia's disdain for Trump continued to grow throughout the four years he served. On occasions, Johnny would mention some of Trump's achievements and try to make her see that not everything he did was a *disaster*, which was the word she usually used about him. She mostly disagreed, and the wall continued to grow between them, but every now and then he could make her budge a bit; she didn't entirely disapprove of The First Step Act, and she could live with the renegotiation of NAFTA, and to some extent she did see the point of the trade war with China. But she hated Johnny when he didn't hate Trump for his diplomacy with North Korea and it was beyond her belief how he could approve of the way Trump's administration rolled back numerous environmental regulations; in time, the withdrawal from the Paris agreement became a more-or-less taboo subject between them; if either one of them said but one word about this withdrawal, it was bound to lead to an argument.

Similarly, the issue of immigration was exceedingly touchy; the travel ban on predominantly Muslim countries made Alicia ask Johnny if he couldn't see what a xenophobic racist Trump was. "A bigot, disguised as a president, who *pretends* to look out for the best interest of his country" was her description of him. Not surprisingly, however, Johnny didn't agree with her on this matter, but he found it difficult to express his opinion. They had plenty of discussions, which revolved around subjects that Alicia knew more about and she was, in general, more articulate than him and often had the upper hand in arguments.

However, Johnny recognized how pivotal the issue of immigration was, and one day decided that he was tired of running out of arguments when he discussed stuff with his wife, wherefore he made a deal with himself to go about it in a more methodical way. It was May 2018, and Trump's "zero tolerance" policy, which led to family separations at the US-Mexico border, had recently been implemented. It was on the news, it was in the papers, and most people were talking at length about it, except for Johnny, who avoided the subject, knowing that nothing good would come from addressing it, at least not with his wife; it was another one of their hot potatoes, and Johnny had decided that he wanted it to remain that way.

In a matter of weeks, it wouldn't be all over the news any longer, and it would be easier to ignore it. Alicia hadn't mentioned it either, and he was certain that she'd decided to go along with the same ignore-it-and-see-if-it-goes-away strategy. Although winning an argument is more fun than losing one, she too was tired of fighting, he thought.

Then one day Alicia was on the phone, and Johnny soon gathered that her father was on the other end. They were talking about the situation at the border, and though Alicia never explicitly encouraged Johnny to be a part of the conversation, she discreetly moved nearer him and slowly raised her voice, so that she eventually stood rather close to him and very audibly told her father what she thought of Trump's way of handling the problems at the border: "It's so inhumane, I don't understand how anyone can support a policy that's so not aligned with our country's values. Think of the impact on these kids and their families. They're gonna be traumatized for years." Johnny was at a stalemate; the words were not really directed at him, so he wasn't supposed to comment on them, but still it was obvious to him what was going on; although she was talking to her father, she wanted her husband to hear what she was saying, and he resented her for it. Why didn't she adhere to their silent agreement of not talking about immigration? This was such a lousy way of getting the last word, he thought; her way of saying, I'm tired of arguing with you, but I need to let you know where I stand on this. Johnny knew that ignoring it would have been the right thing to do; remain unresponsive and give her the satisfaction that she got from his silence. It would be one less fight, which was not a lot, but it was certainly better than one more fight. He resisted the urge to do anything about it for the next two days, but his annoyance didn't diminish, so instead he decided to try to beat his wife at her own game; he spent the next few days searching for arguments in favor of Trump's "zero tolerance" policy and then he memorized these. This was bound to prepare him for a discussion with Alicia, in which he didn't fall short of arguments; it would be his way of showing that his voice mattered too, though he wasn't as scholarly and erudite as her.

Once Johnny had decided to try his little experiment, the sense of knowing that it wasn't the right thing to do was quickly replaced by an almost childish excitement; he looked forward to the battle. He knew that he wasn't necessarily going to win anything in the sense that Alicia wouldn't reconsider her position, but he was expecting an astounded look on her face when those arguments of his kept coming, and that in itself would be a small victory.

It took some time to find the arguments for Johnny, as it proved to be a rather tedious process; first, he googled the words "pro-Trump newspapers" and decided to focus on four newspapers: *New York Post, The Washington Times, The Epoch Times,* and *The Daily Caller.* Second, he had to search for the right articles, and lastly he had to find the right arguments in these articles. He was looking for the right balance between writing down arguments that had some substance to them, while at the same time not being too lengthy for him to understand and memorize. After almost five hours of work, which made him feel like a high school student again, an otherwise unusual feeling for him, his piece of paper read the following:

Strong Deterrent: the "zero tolerance" policy will serve as a strong deterrent to illegal immigration. By implementing strict consequences, fewer people will attempt to cross the border illegally.

Preventing Crime and Terrorism: strict border enforcement is crucial for national security, and Trump's policy will help prevent criminals, drug traffickers, and potential terrorists from entering the country.

Respect for Legal Processes: illegal immigration is unfair to those who go through the legal process to immigrate, and strict enforcement policies will serve to uphold the principle that immigration should be conducted legally and fairly.

Managing Resources: illegal immigration puts a significant strain on public resources, including healthcare, education, and social services. By reducing illegal crossings, these resources can be used for the benefit of American citizens and legal immigrants instead.

When he glanced at his paper, he figured they were all solid arguments, and he decided to wait for the right moment to initiate the discussion, which would be the next time the TV brought attention to the situation at the border. When that happened, Johnny stuck to the plan and told Alicia that he didn't agree with the *critics*—he used a generic word instead of saying *her*—who called Trump's policy inhumane.

Despite not being singled out, Alicia, not surprisingly, caught the bait and immediately argued her case, and, just as expected, she was surprised when she discovered that her husband stood his ground and provided several explanations as to why her way of looking at the whole thing could also be labelled inhumane. It amounted to a fifteen-minutes discussion, and Johnny soon learned that he was right about most of the things that he had anticipated prior to the argument. First of all, he was right about the fact that she wouldn't budge one bit, but he was also right about the fact that that wasn't the most significant thing; feeling empowered after their talk was the important thing.

Secondly, he was right about the fact that deliberately seeking a confrontation like he'd just done was likely not the advisable thing to do; their marital problems didn't begin this day, but they certainly didn't end either; more so than ever before it was frighteningly obvious how much discord there was between them. That in itself was not a good thing, Johnny thought, but at the same time he had to admit to himself that not feeling outsmarted, silenced, and subdued was a nice feeling and instead of toning his newfound strategy down, he turned it up a notch, and in the next two years they had a number of arguments that Johnny was often impressively and aggressively well-prepared for.

*

A couple of hours have passed and a couple of more drinks have been consumed since Alicia promised herself that she wouldn't spend time thinking about how her marriage went from bad to worse from 2016 to 2020, and, realizing that she has done just that, she gathers that she has to uproot herself from the patio, if she's to find the ability to put an end to her trip-down-bad-memories-lane. She gets up and finds herself having to lean on the wall on her way into the house, and once she has stood like this for roughly thirty seconds, she goes upstairs and packs a bag for a trip that doesn't have a destination, a duration, or a purpose. Upon packing enough stuff to get by for at least a couple of days she leaves the house, and briefly considers taking the car, but shuns the thought as she realizes that would not only be too reckless but would also mean having to decide on where to drive the car to. She finds it much easier to trudge down to the train station and jump on the first train to New York City.

During the train ride, she dozes off and doesn't wake up until arriving at Penn Station. She feels dazed as she leaves the train, but also senses that she's starting to sober up, which would normally suit her, but there's nothing normal about this day, so she goes straight to one of the nearest bars to quickly get drunk again.

She momentarily worries about not having a place to stay for the night, and also feels bad about not having told the kids anything about leaving the house, so she calls Jeremy and tells him that an old friend of hers has lost her father and she needs to be there for her.

She still hasn't decided when it will be the right time to tell her children about the divorce; right now, she just attempts to make sure that she doesn't sound drunk, as the purpose of the phone call is to buy herself a couple of days of emancipation. She ignores Johnny's calls, and decides not to return them, knowing that he's not going to ask Gina and Jeremy if they know where their mother is. As for the lack of a hotel room; so be it, she thinks; whatever happens, happens.

It's been quite a few years since Alicia has been in a bar, and this is the first time she has ever set foot in one by herself, so she doesn't know what to expect. She's not a vain woman, but she carries herself with grace and stays fit. Lack of sleep, too many tears, the scruffy jeans and the baggy T-shirt make her appear less attractive than normal, so she decides to spend a few minutes in the ladies' room, whereafter she returns to the bar no longer looking like a woman who is going through the crisis of her life.

Shortly after, a man who introduces himself as Carson offers her a drink, which she willingly accepts. He is loquacious and, in a few minutes, he has already told her that he's not married (probably a lie), lives in New Jersey (probably the truth), is a pilot (definitely a lie) and is forty-three (potentially the truth). From time to time, men in the gym or at work flirt with her, so she's used to it, but flirtation in a bar is different; less subtle, more driven by lust and more goal-oriented. Flirting at work is done to get through the day, flirting in a bar is done to get through the night, and it quickly becomes apparent that Carson is eager to spend the night with her. One drink leads to the next and Alicia likes Carson's company and attention, but when he excuses himself to go to the restroom, she gathers her stuff and leaves the bar, knowing that he will feel perplexed when he returns to two empty bar stools. She considers looking through the windows to behold the look on his face but worries that he might see her, so instead she picks up her pace and walks six blocks to another bar, where she's left to her own company for less than ten minutes before she's offered a drink again.

This time she's offered a drink by a guy who, initially, is not as obviously trying to pick her up. He tells her that he's forty-five, lives close by, and is a surgeon at a nearby hospital, all of which sounds and seems plausible. His name is Anthony, and he comes across as more genuinely interested in Alicia than her friend from before. It seems that he has approached her for the conversation; any flirtation might be a bonus. As a result of this, Alicia ends up spending the better part of three hours in the bar with Anthony, and during this time he consumes two beers and two drinks, and she has three drinks.

By now, Anthony has become less of a gentleman and more of a ladies' man; he compliments her more, leans closer to her, looks her more intently in the eyes, and caresses her body more and more. He has given her no reason to believe that he's married, let alone in a relationship, and nothing he does or says makes her feel uncomfortable. In addition to that, Alicia has begun to notice how other women are checking Anthony out. She gets the impression that he could have chatted up any other female in the bar and relishes the fact that he's having a party with *her*. Even the bartender seems overly flirtatious when she takes his orders.

When Alicia decides to repeat her disappearance act, she does everything exactly like she did a few hours before. The only slight difference is that she's so drunk by now that she doesn't worry about getting caught staring through the windows, so she stands as still as she can on the street and through a tiny window pane sees Anthony returning to the two bar stools that he considered *theirs,* but which are now occupied by two young, Hispanic guys; his first reaction is to proceed to other bar stools, looking searchingly at the empty ones, and he ends up walking around the entire bar, whereupon he pivots and walks in the other direction. He ends up walking around the bar three times before he proceeds to check the booths that are surrounding it.

Eventually Alicia notices him returning to the bar to approach the two young guys. It seems there's a language barrier, but it's obvious that, despite them being Hispanic, they understand *his panic.* Once Anthony realizes that the youngsters cannot help him, he tries to get hold of the bartender. It's evident to Alicia, who has stared through the window for a good five minutes by now, that the bartender tries to take advantage of the situation; she grabs hold of Anthony's cheeks and even tries to place a kiss on his lips, but he turns his right cheek and shortly thereafter steps away from the bar.

Following her peep show, Alicia staggers down the street. She wants to put several blocks behind her, but the drinks are putting pressure on her bladder and she rushes into a bar which is only two blocks away. As she spreads her legs and positions herself on the toilet, she starts to question what she's doing. Is this her way of letting random men know that they *cannot* "grab her by the pussy?" Is this her own, little, private revenge, and if so, does it end now or is this just a build up? She ponders this as she leaves the ladies' room and finds her way to the bar. She orders a beer and notices that it's "Sexual Healing", the sexiest song in the world that fills up the room: "And baby I can't hold it much longer, it's getting stronger and stronger". Alicia starts to regret leaving Anthony behind and feels very alone right now. Luckily for her, a very drunk woman doesn't repulse men in the same manner that very drunk men are likely to repulse women, and in less than ten minutes she's once again in male company: Isaiah, a thirty-two-year-old, Black guy, who lives in Brooklyn and works for the New York fire department.

At this point, Alicia doesn't care if *he* is telling the truth, because she's not; she's telling the truth about where she lives and what she does for a living but doesn't say a word about being married, or being about to get a divorce, or having two kids. As they dive further into conversation, Alicia thinks that Isaiah looks even younger than his age, although now she cannot tell if she's only arriving at this conclusion because she's more drunk than she's been in years. Drunk or not, she admires his athletic look and when she indiscreetly touches his biceps and chest, the carved-in-wood impression leaves her with a burning sensation in her pants. Shortly before the bar closes, Isaiah excuses himself and when he returns from the restroom, Alicia, who hasn't disappeared this time, tells him that she either has to find a hotel or follow him into the night. Less than an hour after, she finds herself in Isaiah's apartment in Brooklyn; roughly twenty years ago she had sex for the first time in this borough, and now she has sex with the second guy in her life in more-or-less the same place. She was drunk then, and she's drunk now, and she fucks him and lets him fuck her in ways that are wilder than anything she has ever tried. It's not a particularly lengthy intercourse but it's cathartic and when they wake up, their impulses get the better of them and they go at it again. When she leaves his apartment around noon, they exchange phone numbers, and although she doubts she will ever see him again, she appreciates the fact that it would be possible to get in touch with Isaiah again; right now, he's the only man she can think of who can grab her by the pussy.

During the subway ride back to Manhattan, it dawns on Alicia that she still doesn't have the faintest idea what her plan is. She's tired and thirsty, her muscles ache, and her blood pressure is increased. She experiences a sensitivity to light and sound but is also fascinated by the bustling life that plays out in front of her. The subway car is an oxymoronic mix of the closest thing to a home for homeless people and a fashion show on wheels at the same time; old, dirty men with no teeth sit next to beautiful, young women sporting sequin dresses, raffia bags, and Mary Jane flats.

At Bleecker Street station, a young woman, probably half Alicia's age, places a tote bag on her lap as she sits down next to Alicia. It has "Yale Law School" written on it, and for a moment Alicia cannot take her eyes off the bag and becomes almost lachrymose. Since she doesn't have a destination, she decides to get off at the next stop, and as the train begins to slow, she puts her hand on the young woman's shoulder and wishes her good luck with her studies, and, when she gets up from her seat, she also wishes her all the best in life. "Thanks, you too," the young woman says, "but the bag isn't mine." Alicia doesn't hear the last part, and shortly after she finds herself on the streets of SoHo and checks into the nearest hotel.

After a nap, which, strangely enough, makes her hangover worse, she not only musters the energy to climb into the bathtub but also to masturbate; a strange way of washing off last night's experience while at the same time commemorating it. After reaching her climax, Alicia stays in the tub for an hour whereafter she gets ready to go out for a bite to eat.

She returns to the hotel at eight o'clock and then decides that she can no longer postpone the unpostponable, so she calls Gina—she tried Jeremy first, but his phone went straight to voicemail—and tells her that she will leave New York in the morning and asks her to find out whether her and Jeremy can be at home tomorrow night as she needs to speak to both of them.

It's the hardest phone call she has made in her life, and she knows that their talk tomorrow night is going to be even harder; she hates Johnny for putting her in this situation but insists that the kids need to hear about the divorce from *her*. She's temporarily relieved by the fact that Gina didn't ask her what she needs to talk to them about, as that gives her another twenty-four hours to find out how she wants to break it to the kids, but just as quickly becomes distressed by the fact that she *only* has twenty-four hours to find this out. She spends an hour playing out the conversation in her head and trying to imagine their reaction, but eventually realizes that she doesn't have a clue as to how they'll react. Upon this, she starts looking at pictures and videos from last night. She barely remembers the intercourse, nor the filming of it; Johnny and she never filmed each other during intimate hours, and she has never watched porn, and watched only relatively few movies with sex scenes—she always found it awkward—so watching a sex video with *herself* and a man who's a complete stranger is an immensely unusual experience for her. She almost feels as if it's a different woman who's moaning and groaning on the screen. She feels tired, hungover, sad, satisfied, nauseated, ashamed, elated, and proud at the same time, and on top of all these conflicting emotions, she feels vindictive, and considers sending the video to Johnny. She particularly wants him to see the part where she goes down on Isaiah, as this is where it most obviously shows that his dick is much bigger than Johnny's.

Alicia's finger is resting on the *send* button, but she restrains herself and puts the phone down without sending anything, since something inside her tells her that sharing this blow job with her soon-to-be-ex-husband is too much of a low blow. Instead, she watches the video one last time whereafter she considers deleting it, her finger moves very close to the trash can icon on the phone, but she decides to save the video and finally surrenders to her fatigue.

On her way back to Cold Spring, Alicia texts Johnny and lets him know that she needs the house to herself, since she intends to tell the kids about the divorce tonight. She's anxious during the train ride, and the subsequent afternoon feels like an eternity despite the fact that she tries to kill as much time as possible by buying groceries and cooking dinner. Gina and Jeremy are at the house by six o'clock and, as dinner is ready, the three of them just sit down to eat right away. The meal isn't spent in silence, but Alicia decides to wait until afterwards to mention the divorce, seeing as neither Gina nor Jeremy ask her what she wanted to talk to them about; she almost gets the impression that Gina has forgotten their phone call from last night, and considers calling off the whole thing, but then, after dinner when they are all in the living room, Alicia goes to the bathroom, slaps herself a couple of times on both cheeks, and then returns to the living room to initiate the talk.

"Can you put your phones down, guys?" Alicia says and feels tears swelling up inside of her. "Like I said last night, I wanted to talk to you about something." She does as much as she can to suppress the tears, knowing that neither Gina nor Jeremy can cry if she's crying. Nevertheless, the tiniest tear in the world finds its way to her cheek, and since both of the kids have put their phones down by now, she carries on: "I hate having to tell you this, and I don't know how to say it, so I'm just gonna say it like it is; your father and I are getting a divorce." A bit to her surprise, neither of the kids says anything initially, so she continues, "We haven't sorted out the details yet, but we will do that very soon."

"What do you mean by details?" Gina asks.

"Well, first of all, we have to find out if one of us can stay in the house, I guess, or if we both have to move."

"You *guess?*"

"Yes, I *guess,*" Alicia says and immediately regrets saying the word in the same passive-aggressive manner as her daughter. "I mean, I haven't tried this before, and I haven't had the time to talk that much to your father."

"Your *father,*" Gina fumes. "You can just call him Dad like we've done the last nineteen years. And what do you mean you haven't had the time to talk to *Dad;* but you had the time to run off to New York to help some friend through her crisis. Or was that a lie?"

Alicia doesn't answer her daughter's question right away, and feels temporarily saved by Jeremy, who now speaks up for the first time.

"What happened, Mom, tell us?"

"He cheated on me." She continues her struggle to hold back her tears, and still more-or-less succeeds, although more than one tiny tear rolls down her cheeks this time. "I think that's all you need to know about it." She'd already decided that she would prefer that they know as little as possible, so she remains silent, waiting to see how many questions she'll now need to answer.

"With whom?" Gina says.

"I don't know. Not someone I know, just some strange *woman.*" Alicia sticks to singular, though she's tempted to use the plural form.

"How do you know it's true?"

"Well, I found out by accident. Trust me, Gina, you don't wanna know the details. He didn't intend to tell me, but he doesn't deny it."

After a moment of silence, Gina gets up and leaves the living room. Alicia notices that she's misty-eyed, but so is Jeremy, and her maternal instincts are conflicted; should she get up and comfort her daughter or stay in the room and comfort her son? She cannot do the right thing here, but doing nothing would be the most wrong thing to do, so she moves closer to her son, puts her arm around his shoulders, and lets him know that everything will be okay.

"I know, I just hadn't seen it coming. And I feel sorry for you," he says and finally adds, "For both of you."

Their moment is interrupted by Gina, who returns to the living room and asks where her *dad* is. Alicia says she's not sure, but that she suspects that he's spending the night at work. She encourages her daughter to sit down next to her, which she does, a bit surprisingly to Alicia. By now, Gina is bawling her eyes out, and Alicia yanks her close so that she can put her arms around both her children. She keeps repeating that things will be fine and continues to succeed in holding back her tears, thereby leaving room for theirs. Right now, that's the best and only thing she can do for them, she thinks.

Once the kids have gone to bed, Alicia decides to send a message to Johnny. Texting is not appropriate for the situation, so she gets her computer and prepares an email. She knows that they will need to see each other and sort out a lot of details, but apart from that she really wants the house to herself, which is basically what she wants him to know. She doesn't know how to begin the email; *dear* is certainly the wrong word, and so is *hi* or *hello*, or any other greeting, so she just jumps right into it:

I know we have a lot of things to sort out, first of all the housing situation, but right now I just need to know that I have the house to myself while we work everything out. I'll let you know when I'm not here, and I'll make sure not to be here all the time, so you can see the kids. For starters, I will need a few more days and then I'll reach out to you again. Alicia.

She briefly considers whether she's pushing it by letting him know that she wants him out of the house but then remembers Saturday night, and also thinks about the conversation she's just had with their kids, and assures herself that she's making the right decision. Besides, it's not like she's leaving him without a roof over his head. He probably doesn't have any friends he can stay with, because he has been busy fucking foreigners in the past years, but he can spend the nights at work or live with his parents. When she pushes the *send* button, she feels slightly relieved, and goes to bed thinking that maybe she was telling her children the truth; maybe things will work out.

Chapter six
Joseph Robinette Biden, Jr.

Johnny's back hurts, his neck and shoulder are in pain, and he feels an overwhelming sense of muscle stiffness as he gets on his feet and goes to take a piss. The lousy mattress can't be blamed entirely for his discomfort, but obviously it doesn't help. He checks the time when he returns to the office, which is his bedroom for the night, and as he realizes that it's a quarter past four in the morning, he tries to fall asleep again, which, however, quickly proves futile.

After tossing and turning on the mattress for almost an hour, he gets up and cleans the office. He removes the six empty beer bottles and the half-eaten pizza, and opens all windows for at least an hour, as he wants to make sure that his father doesn't catch the smell from the five cigarettes that he smoked before he went to sleep.

It's been less than twelve hours since he told his parents that he's getting a divorce and is intending to spend at least the first couple of nights at the office, while he's trying to figure out his living arrangements. He doesn't mind them knowing that he's feeling downhearted and insecure about the future, he doesn't even mind them knowing that he'll be inclined to use alcohol to numb his emotions in the nights to come, as long as he can maintain a proper appearance at work, but he doesn't want them to know that he has started smoking cigarettes again; a habit he had quit almost twenty years ago, when his twins were born.

As Johnny gets up, his body reminds him how cigarettes add to the feeling of a hangover; his mouth is extremely dry, he's dizzy, and his heartbeat is faster than normal. Six beers alone cannot have done this much damage to him, and it's a good thing that he has at least a couple of hours before he has to open Smith's Carmarket.

He positions himself in the office chair, which is so ergonomic that he considers whether it would actually have provided him with a better night's sleep than the mattress on the floor, which, by now, is the only thing in the office that reveals that he has spent the night in there.

It's pointless to try to fall asleep again but he will test his hypothesis about the chair tonight, he decides. In the meantime, he grabs his phone and turns on the news which tells him that, "President Biden will be joined by care workers and unions as he lays out how he will build on progress with transformational investments in child care, home care, paid family and medical leave, tax cuts for workers and families, and other priorities, which are fully paid for by making the wealthy and big corporations pay their fair share in taxes. That is in sharp contrast with congressional Republicans, who would make devastating cuts to funding for care, healthcare, Social Security, and Medicare to pay for massive tax cuts for billionaires and big corporations."

Typical Biden, Johnny thinks, and while social policy and tax policy are not issues that he himself is overly interested in, he cannot help but dwell on it, since it reminds him of not only his wife, but also his parents-in-law.

He imagines the three of them sitting around the kitchen table reassuring themselves, with echoing voices, that these policies are so right for this country. He likely wouldn't be invited into the conversation, and if he were, or if he tried to join their talk, they would leave him with the impression that he was butting in; like a school kid who enters a discussion that he isn't mature enough to grasp.

He remembers how he had once memorized a line that he had read in a newspaper: "The expansion of social programs, such as childcare, paid leave, and healthcare, could create dependency on government assistance and reduce incentives to work." He tended to agree with the statement, but when he shared it with Alicia and her parents, they accused him of not caring enough for the weakest individuals in society, which he thought was a misinterpretation of "his" words.

Then they went on about the advantages of Biden's Build Back Better Act, and though he had tried to be prepared, it was too detailed for him, and whenever he wasn't set for a talk like that, the discussion would quickly come to a halt.

More often than not, if Johnny wasn't prepared for it, a conversation like the one in the kitchen would end with him pretending that he had a phone call to make or excusing himself to go to the restroom, where he spent as much time as he possibly could without it seeming too weird; sometimes he'd spend close to ten minutes in there before returning to the others hoping that they would have moved on to a new subject.

As Johnny sits in the office chair this morning, hungover, sleep-deprived, and dejected, he tries to tell himself that if he were to find something positive in his current situation, it would be the fact that he doesn't have to put up with his wife and her family through one more Biden vs. Trump election campaign. It's not that Johnny has that much against Biden, whom he considers less elitist than most of his party members, and Johnny also acknowledges that he has a connection with and an understanding for the working class; an average Joe, who understands the average American.

Likewise, Johnny isn't too preoccupied with Biden's age, or the fact that he stumbles over words or mumbles. Obviously, he doesn't agree with very many of Biden's policies, but at the same time he doesn't think that he's a president who is damaging the country. He finds him immensely boring, but that's about the worst thing he can think of when it comes to the forty-sixth president of the United States of America.

In some ways, Johnny would almost be willing to go as far as saying that Biden has done a good job and pushed the nation in a better direction; Johnny had, for instance, begun to acknowledge Biden's effort to implement reasonable gun laws, not only when he served as Obama's vice president but also in recent years as president.

Johnny's father liked hunting and therefore he grew up in a home with firearms and did believe in an individual's right to protect oneself, one's family and one's property. He had never owned a gun as an adult, but that was simply because he was a person who never felt unsafe and therefore had never considered buying one. In the first years of their marriage, gun laws were something that Alicia and Johnny rarely talked about.

They both liked to keep it that way, and since Johnny never expressed an interest in buying any type of firearms—he knew Alicia would object to that—it was fairly easy for them to avoid the subject.

Naturally, the Sandy Hook shooting, and other tragedies close to that scale, were not ignored completely between the two of them, and after the kids started elementary school, it had also become increasingly difficult for them to skirt the topic, but, for once, they managed to focus on what they agreed on; that having to expose five-year-olds to ALICE training is absurd, and the expression "age-appropriate school shooting training" is equally absurd.

As long as they didn't talk specifically about the Second Amendment or the implementation of actual gun laws, they were fine. Yet the older Gina and Jeremy got, the more questions they started asking, and the Santa Fe High School tragedy in particular seemed to impact them.

The tragedy occurred almost 1,700 miles from their home, so using the word "traumatized" would probably be pushing it a bit, but the kids did spend the summer asking a lot of questions about the Second Amendment, the difference between federal and state laws, guns laws in New York, the NRA, the expression "the only way to stop a bad guy with a gun is with a good guy with a gun", the sixty-vote threshold, profiles of school shooters, pistols, shotguns, AR-15-style weapons, high capacity magazines, red flag laws, background checks, open carry, concealed carry, and what not.

Jeremy and Alicia didn't always agree on what to answer, so they made a pact; when it comes to this, we'll answer the kids with facts, not opinions; it's okay to explain to them what the Second Amendment is, but avoid sharing what we think of it.

After Gina and Jeremy started high school, and, just as their parents had noticed that the kids had stopped talking about school shootings for a while, the topic came up again as they told their parents that they had been given an open assignment in English class, in which they had to comment on the issue of school shootings.

The teacher had made it very clear that the assignment was indeed *open*; the students could account for the problems with school shootings in the US since Columbine, analyze the factors that cause school shootings, comment on the solutions proposed in the gun debate, or discuss whether it's realistic that there will be fewer school shootings in the US in the future.

They could also choose a more personal approach, i.e., an interview with someone who had experienced a school shooting or they could describe their own concerns and nightmares on the topic.

Neither Gina nor Jeremy was in the habit any longer of sharing all their school assignments with their parents, but since this particular task was their first ever in high school, they both decided to show it to them upon completion.

Gina went first, and said that she had attempted to write a short story in the first-person narrative, and she exuded pride when she laid her story before her parents' eyes:

Running for your life
By
Gina Smith Vanderbilt

The first thing I do when I wake up is check my schedule. Nothing is canceled, so there are six lessons on my schedule today. Two P.E. lessons, two English lessons, and two US history lessons. This means that Sarah, my best friend who is giving me a ride to school, will be here in less than an hour, so I must get ready. I don't have to shower because the P.E. lessons are the first on our schedule.

Currently we are doing track and field, and Sarah, who always seems to know things a little bit before me, says she has heard that we have to choose between jumping, running, or throwing today, and she tells me that she will sign up for jumping activities, because she's tired of running.

I tell her about my 5K run with my father the other day; how it was the turning point of my day, and how I think that running is good for me at the moment and that I've actually thought about trying to do a 10K run soon, so running in P.E. will make for good practice. We take turns guessing which activity our closest friends will sign up for, and the rest of the drive is spent in unusual, but not awkward, silence.

As always, Sarah is right; Mrs. Renfro, our P.E. teacher, starts the lesson by dividing us into three groups. I, and eleven other students, have chosen running. We're told to go to the running track where the teacher's aide will initiate a Cooper test. Once we get there, the rubberized, artificial surface feels comforta-

ble under my feet. I try to do the math in my head; based on my running performance the day before yesterday I should be able to cover about one and a half mile in twelve minutes, since the distance is much shorter, and I expect to be able to increase my pace.

After the obligatory warm-up exercises, the teacher's aide starts the test, and I quickly learn that about half of the runners seem faster than me and the other half seem slower.

After the first three minutes I have a solid rhythm and a pace that seems suitable for the remainder of the test. There will probably even be room for a little sprint towards the end. Halfway through the test I still feel good, but then, just like the day before yesterday when I was running with my father, I suddenly start to imagine myself as someone who's escaping from a school shooter. The thought does not evaporate from my mind as quickly as the other day, so, while doing the best I can to keep up my pace, I start to look around.

"Focus on your own test, and forget about the others," the teacher's aide says to me, as I pass him one more time. He obviously assumes that I'm looking backwards to check whether the ones behind me are catching up on me.

The running track is about 440 yards, so it's a matter of time before I pass him again. I slowly start to focus on my test again as I conclude that there's nothing to be scared of. No matter where I look, I can only see five runners in front of me, six runners behind me, and the teacher's aide with the watch in his hand. But then, as I approach the bleachers, I see a shadow lurking beneath the seats. I'm approaching the bleachers relative-

ly quickly and I'm pretty exhausted by now, so I'm merely able to get a glimpse of the shadow when I pass by the bleachers. It's a male, and his age is impossible for me to zoom in on.

If it hadn't been for the running, I would have felt my heart starting to pound faster, and the anxiety tightening its grip on me, but I'm too exhausted to succumb to this, and ten seconds later I've put several yards between myself and the shadow beneath the bleachers.

As I realize that nothing has happened, I take a breath which is as deep as my exhaustion allows me to. Relief is temporary, however, as I quickly realize that I will be passing the bleachers once again in less than three minutes. I consider faking an injury and quitting the test when I'm on the opposite side to the bleachers. Then I could watch the bleachers from afar and warn the others if necessary. I also consider telling the teacher's aide, who's less than fifty yards ahead of me by now, that there's a man underneath the bleachers.

I even consider leaving the running track and running as far away as I possibly can. For some reason I end up doing none of these things and every step ends up bringing me closer to the bleachers, until I'm finally close enough to notice that the shadow, whom I can now make out as a chubby, middle-aged man with gray and thinning hair, has stepped out and positioned himself close to a fence.

The man is standing with his back to the running track and appears to be looking for something in his jeans. He looks over the shoulder and seems to be paying close attention to all the runners, as if trying to no-

tice when we are as close to him as possible. Seconds later, I see him putting his right hand inside the waistband of his trousers and he's obviously trying to pull something out. It must be a gun and I don't know whether to throw myself on the ground, hide behind the bleachers, or run in the opposite direction, so I continue moving forward despite the fact that every step brings me closer to my own death.

I'm just about to turn my head and warn the ones behind me, either by screaming that there's a gunman behind the bleachers or by waving my hands frantically as if trying to tell them not to proceed, but in less than two seconds I drop that thought as the man has begun to urinate through the fence. Relief once again washes through me as I pass the bleachers and I check my watch to learn how much time there's left of the test.

Once I approach the bleachers again, for what will be my last round in this test, I notice that the middle-aged man is now sitting on the bleachers. As I get closer, it becomes obvious that he's following me with his eyes. His head is clearly moving slowly from the left to the right side at the exact pace with which I'm passing him. I do the only thing that I feel I can do in this situation; I pick up my pace and finish with a sprint so impressive that I manage to catch up with two runners who had been way ahead of me earlier in the race.

The teacher's aide calls all of us over and once we're gathered in a corner of the running track, he starts to jot down our test results in his book. "Pretty good. Now you know which distance to beat next time," he says, before touching upon stuff like maximum oxygen consumption and red, slow, oxidative muscle cells.

I get distracted, however, as the middle-aged man starts to approach our huddle. He's walking straight towards us, and I start to quiver. He's so close that I mistakenly convince myself that it would be pointless trying to escape if he starts shooting, so instead I almost adopt the behavior of an animal that pretends to be dead when faced with danger; I put my head down and stare into the grass and notice the beads of sweat dropping from my forehead.

I remain seated like this until I hear the two girls next to me whispering to each other. "He's such a pervert, that guy. I've seen him before, eyeing the girls during P.E.," the first girl says. "Yikes. What is he, like fifty or something? He reminds me of my neighbor, who's always checking me out and chatting me up. It's totally grossing me out," the second girl says. Just like a couple of minutes ago, relief washes through me as I once again realize that I was wrong about the chubby man. "I think I'm gonna put on loose clothing next time," the first girl says.

"No way. I ain't doing that. Don't let that jackass decide that." Once the second girl says that, I think for the first time about my own clothing. I'm wearing tight training pants and a tight sports bra, but I don't think I'm going to change into something loose next time; I think I agree with the second girl on that. I just know that in some peculiar way this is the first time in my life that I have felt relieved because a man, who is probably three times as old as me, checked me out. If I ever see him again, I can remind myself that he's disgusting, but he's not a killer.

It took a surprisingly long time for her parents to read the story and Gina sensed that her tale really got under their skin. She's less academic than her brother, but quickly detected that from her parents' perspective this was a give-credit-where-credit-is-due situation; they complimented her way of building suspense in the story and told her that her spelling and writing had improved significantly.

Basically, it was just a job well done, they said, which was nice for her to hear, since they were going to read her brother's assignment afterwards, and it would probably be even better.

When her father put the papers down and looked pityingly at her, she could tell that it would be a good idea to assure him that it was a *creative* writing task; the story was made up and she told her father that she wouldn't have feared anything in a similar situation, and while it was true that the story was made up, it wasn't true that she wouldn't have feared anything in a similar situation.

When everything was said about Gina's assignment, Jeremy took his paper out of the school bag and laid it on the kitchen table in front of his parents. He told them that he had described a nightmare, and having paid attention to his sister's assurances, decided to tell his parents beforehand that his story was also made up.

He said that although of course he occasionally worried about school shootings, it wasn't something that he had nightmares about; however, the last part was a lie. "But read it and weep," he said, and then his mother picked up the papers and began reading.

Pandemonium
By
Jeremy Smith Vanderbilt

I'm having lunch with my friends, and we're talking about last night's Knicks game, but our conversation comes to a halt as we suddenly hear six popping sounds. They echo, they are very, very sharp and they are the loudest sound I've ever heard. Seconds later the cafeteria is in pandemonium. I see students running in every possible direction, screaming at the top of their lungs. There's a moment when panic paralyzes me and I'm incapable of moving, but someone grabs my arm and shortly after I start running.

The cafeteria is noisy by now, but it's impossible not to hear how the popping sounds continue. At one point there's a brief pause, but then very shortly after, the sounds reoccur. I haven't seen a shooter and I'm not even sure a lot of the other students have; everyone just seems to be running away from the sounds, though not really being able to detect where the noise is coming from.

It's highly probable that everyone in the cafeteria has trained for this. I have trained for situations like this many times. I know where the exits are, I know how to open windows, how to break windows, and how to use fire escapes and access ladders. No matter where I am at my school, I've received training in exiting the premises as quickly as possible in case of an emergency. I should be able to find the nearest way out with the speed of a bullet, to save me from being hit by a bullet.

We all should. But training is one thing, and this is something else completely.

As soon as everyone knows that this is not a drill, there's panic everywhere. In my attempt to exit the cafeteria, I bump into other students, because no one remembers where the nearest exit is, and the same thing happens everywhere in the cafeteria, so everyone ends up spending more time in there than necessary. The popping sounds keep coming but as some students have been able to leave the premises and are probably heading for the school's designated gathering place, the cafeteria has been emptied to the point that it's no longer as easy for the shooter to hide among the many students and use the chaos to blend in.

*At some point, the shooting stops once again and then I catch a glimpse of the shooter. He's reloading, which he obviously manages to do very quickly. He pivots around, probably to detect where the biggest groups of students are, before he decides to stand still, facing in my direction. We're separated by less than ten feet and his arm is facing so precisely in my direction that if I ran straight ahead I would run right into the barrel of his gun. My body is incapable of moving, which gives him the easiest opportunity in the world for a point-blank shot. I'm looking at him with eyes that are begging for mercy, but the eyes facing mine are as dead as the many bodies lying around him. This is it! He is going to kill me. **HE** is going to kill me. He **IS GOING TO KILL** me. He is going to kill **ME!***

And the next thing I'm thinking is that I want my parents to be here. I want to hold my mom's hands, and I want my dad to help me dodge the bullets or attack the shooter and turn the shooter's gun at him instead and kill him so that this madness stops before more innocent lives are spilled. *And then suddenly I feel my mother's arm grabbing mine and I ask how she got here so quickly. I'm sobbing and I keep repeating the words "How did you get here so quickly?" and it takes me a while to register that she came because she heard me screaming.*

Every time I ask her how she got here she says that she came because she heard me screaming, but it makes no sense to me. What was she doing at my school on a normal Monday during lunch break? Had she somehow heard that there was a shooter at my school before the shooter entered the cafeteria, and then my mother arrived just in time to rescue me, and does this mean that there are more dead bodies all over the school, or does it mean that there's more than one shooter?

My mother begins to gently shake me, and I start to come to my senses. I look around and see my desk, my closet, and my pictures on the wall. I touch myself, and my mother, to check for gunshot wounds, while realizing that this is not necessary, because no one has been shot. It was just a terrible nightmare. It's two-thirty in the morning and I'm in my bed and my mom is sitting by my side and I'm as safe as I can possibly be. I'm in an upright position now and I apologize to my mom for waking her up, which she of course doesn't care about. She asks if I can go back to sleep and I say that I'm not sure, but insist that she does because she has to get up early for work. I feel tired as soon as she leaves my room, but it still takes about an hour before I fall asleep.

Again, both Alicia and Johnny applauded their child for an "outstanding effort," and while they did mean what they said, Jeremey still sensed that they, for once, considered Gina's work better. It wasn't an issue for him; on the contrary, since he was typically the overachiever of the two, he found it nice that his sister could also shine every once in a while. He actually hoped that she'd picked up the same vibe as he did; that they found her assignment slightly better than his.

Even though both children had understated the extent to which they tended to worry about school shootings, reading their assignments was still an eye-opener for Johnny. There were certainly those who were more staunch defenders of the Second Amendment than him, but at the same time he had shared Trump's concern that if you let Biden put a ban on assault weapons, then it would be a matter of time before Biden would also try to put a ban on handguns and hunting rifles; and although Johnny had always been in favor of the former, he had never been in favor of the latter; a sentiment which slowly started to change the day he read "Running For Your Life" and "Pandemonium" and afterwards looked into his children's eyes, and maybe, just maybe, knew that they were lying to him when they said that the stories weren't about their own concerns.

Either way, it got to the point where Johnny considered the Bipartisan Safer Communities Act a huge victory, one that he even celebrated and didn't mind giving Biden credit for, and in the following days he even heard himself saying that the next, logical step in the fight against gun violence would be a ban on firearms; *all* firearms, he even said, and for one, brief, shiny moment, there was actually something, in those days in the end of June 2022, that Johnny and his wife and her parents could agree on.

By now, it's almost nine o'clock and Johnny finds it difficult to get up from the ergonomic office chair despite knowing that his father will arrive within a few minutes, as they need to get the auto shop ready. It was a shock to him that he was exposed, exposed himself, for the cheater that he is, and it's an added shock that he's now facing a divorce. He knows their marriage was dysfunctional in plenty of ways, but if a divorce has to happen, he would have preferred it to happen after the children moved out of the house. However, as he finally gets up from the chair, he tries to tell himself that it's all water under the bridge now and that things will fall into place. For now, he just has to open the store, put on a customer-friendly smile, and make sure that he shows his father that he can still fulfill his duties at work.

Nine hours later, it's mission accomplished for Johnny; he has gotten through the day and though it was busy, his father did have time to notice that Johnny's work was beyond reproach; he even managed to sell four cars, which is twice as much as can be expected on a normal day at Smith's Carmarket. As they're closing up the store, the father asks Johnny to sit down for a minute. Henry is a taciturn and reticent man and Johnny knows that asking him to sit down is his dad's way of showing that he cares; things that are said after someone has asked you to "Have a seat" are more significant than those said while standing up.

Even though it's a short chat, which amounts to hardly anything than a father letting his son know that he hopes he'll be okay, as Henry doesn't have the vocabulary to express anything beyond that, Johnny appreciates it and assures his father that he'll be fine. He then declines his father's dinner invitation and as soon as Henry has left the office, Johnny goes for a walk to clear his mind. He thinks about how quaint and idyllic Cold Spring is; set against the backdrop of the Hudson Highlands, the village offers stunning views of the river and surrounding mountains, and as he continues his walk down the picturesque Main Street, with its antique shops, boutique stores and cozy cafes, he notices how well-preserved many of these nineteenth century buildings in his hometown are.

It's not that he's normally blind to these things, but he seizes upon it more today, and reflects on the privilege of living on the banks of the Hudson River. Within the first hour of his walk, he sees five pregnant women, which reminds him just how family-friendly his community is, and he passes several families on his way; dads carrying their sons on their shoulders, moms pushing trolleys, dads holding their daughters' hands, moms holding their sons' hands, families of four forming a line and all holding hands, grandparents gathered around a restaurant table with their children and grandchildren, parents having a barbeque in the garden with their four kids, all of which reminds Johnny of the life that he has and hasn't had. He wipes a tear from his cheek and returns to the office around eight o'clock.

From there, he calls Gina, tells her that he misses her, and says that he's sorry for causing her so much pain. He levels with her and says that he doesn't know if he will move back into the house but promises that he will do whatever he can to ensure a speedy process in terms of arranging the living situation. He tells her that he's staying at his parents' place.

When she was a kid, Gina spent a lot of time at the auto shop, and even today she still regularly stops by, so although he knows that she likes the place, he also knows that she doesn't think of it as a place where you can spend the night. He rounds off by ensuring her that everything will fall into place and promises to call her again tomorrow.

One down, one to go, he thinks and gets ready to call Jeremy, as this is not a let-your-brother-know-what-I-just-said call. Before dialing Jeremy's number, he grabs a beer and a cigarette, his first of the evening. Johnny gives a sigh of relief when his son's phone goes straight to voicemail, and since he doesn't know whether Jeremy gets a notification that says that he has missed a call, he texts him and lets him know that he will try calling again tomorrow. He then finishes his beer and his cigarette, and considers having one more of each, but his tiredness gets the better of him and he falls asleep in the ergonomic office chair.

Chapter seven
Thomas Matthew Crooks

It's early in the morning when Gina wakes up, and she hopes Liam, her boyfriend, will soon open his eyes. She knows she won't see him for a couple of days when she leaves his house, so she caresses his torso, and when that doesn't work, she places a gentle kiss on his lips, which, however, doesn't have an effect either; he's still snoozing. She then places her right hand in his groin area, initially on top of his boxer shorts, and then, when that seemingly has some sort of effect, she moves her hand inside his boxer shorts. When she looks at his face, it appears that while he might not be in dreamland anymore, he's not really awake either. Gina spends a few seconds enjoying the sight of Liam's morning wood, and then takes it one step further and puts his dick in her mouth, which finally makes him come alive and then shortly after Gina has already given her boyfriend a hand-job and a blowjob, and has been on her back and on top of her boyfriend, and it's not even eight o'clock in the morning. Afterwards, they spend another half an hour in bed before they go downstairs for breakfast and act really drowsily to make Liam's parents believe that they just woke up.

Liam and Gina have been going out for a year, and since their mother told her about the divorce, which is a little more than three months ago, she has spent most of her time at his place, not only because she has preferred it that way, but also because his parents have made it abundantly clear that they understand her situation and told her that she can stay as long as she likes. After breakfast, they return to Liam's room where they unwind for about an hour and then Gina packs her bag and leaves.

As soon as she has left Liam's doorstep, she sends Jeremy a snap and lets him know that she'll be *there* in a few minutes—she cannot use the word *home* about that place anymore. Admittedly, her mother has done everything in her power to make things as smooth as possible in recent weeks, but her childhood house has become an unhomely home, and the main reason she's going to spend the weekend there is that her mother has promised Jeremy and her that they have the house to themselves the entire weekend, and while Gina looks forward to spending an entire weekend with her brother, she would have preferred any other location.

Jeremy snaps Gina back right away telling her that he's already *there*—he uses the same word as Gina, though he doesn't, to the same extent as her, have an aversion against the word *home*—and that he looks forward to seeing her. Since Liam's house is just a mile away from their parents' house, Gina and Jeremy are reunited shortly after. They exchange extended hugs before they sit down and spend a couple of hours catching up. Although they have seen each other on and off for the past three months, they both feel that they have somehow drifted apart; Gina has avoided spending too much time in the house—sometimes she hasn't been there for a week at a time—and whenever she has been there, they haven't really had time to catch up. Initially, they take turns telling each other about work; they are both pushing towards the end of a gap year, and Jeremy, who's working as an administrative assistant and doing some tutoring on the side, says that things are going fine but that at the same time he looks forward to starting his sociology studies at Columbia University after the summer.

Gina is proud of her brother; making it into an Ivy League school is a tremendous effort and she acknowledges and admires the effort that he has put into fulfilling his dream. She's past the point of weighing herself against her brother and has made peace with the idea that he will likely become the wealthier of the two; therefore, it doesn't bug her to talk about her own life, which entails working as a barista at a local café. She's not even ashamed to admit that it's been increasingly difficult for her to make ends meet in the past three months without her parents providing for her.

Despite the hospitality of Liam's parents, she doesn't want to be an overstayer, so she's also spent more time with her friends and there's a limit to the number of take-out and restaurant meals that you can afford on a barista's salary. Gina doesn't mind this hand-to-mouth lifestyle but is still counting down the days—as of this day, she needs to count another forty-six days—until she starts a new chapter in her life, in the program to become a medical assistant at CUNY Bronx Community College.

When it's almost noon, Gina and Jeremy both know that the chit-chat will soon come to an end. The past couple of hours have been nice for both of them; they're not close-knit twins, but they do share a bond that extends beyond that of most siblings, and there's a sense of *twintuition* between them that makes them know, without having to say it with words, that they need to get into the difficult part; the real reason why they are there. A little past noon, Gina initiates this part.

"So, Dad's getting a new place to live, huh?" It's not clear to Jeremy whether it's an actual question or just an exclamation, which Gina intends to elaborate on, but since she doesn't continue, he feels obligated to reply. "Guess so, that's probably for the better. He told me about a week ago, and I haven't spoken to him since. What do you know about the place?"

"Probably not a lot more than you. It's in Cornwall-On-Hudson and it's a two-bedroom apartment, but I think he said that it's just a little more than 600 square feet, so the kitchen and the living room must be really tiny."

"I guess. We almost couldn't fit our living room into his entire apartment," Jeremy says, and notices that Gina is neither close to laughing nor smiling at his comment. "But I hope that he can adjust to apartment life, it must be quite an … *upheaval*." Despite never having heard the word before, Gina says that she agrees.

"But I think it's the right thing for him. He used to live in an apartment before he met Mom, and they lived there until we were, like, three years old. He'll adapt, besides, it's probably a good idea to put a river between the two of them."

"For his sake or for her sake?"

"Mainly for his sake. Doesn't Mom hate him?"

"I don't know if she hates him as much as she did when she found out that he was cheating. I mean, it's not like she thinks they should get back together, but she seems more … *appeased*."

"God, will you knock it off with the fancy words," Gina says. "I'm not a soon-to-be-Columbia University student." They both laugh and Jeremy says that he will watch his language.

He continues, "Anyway, it's not something that we're talking about, and maybe she's just adapting to the situation. It was just a vibe I got, that maybe Mom was starting to see that their marriage was so bad that it's for the best that it ended."

"But she's pissed at him for cheating, isn't she?" Gina considers saying that she suspects their mother is just pretending to be more at ease about the whole thing but decides to remain silent.

"She is. Shouldn't she be?"

"She should, but …" Gina doesn't know how to continue that sentence.

"Everything before *but* is bullshit."

"Ha ha, good one. What I'm trying to say is that I agree with you; of course Dad should never have cheated on Mom. That's always wrong, but I think I understand why he did it."

"Why?"

"Well, like you said; it's probably gonna end up being for the best. I mean, it's not like they're arguing all the time, but they disagree on everything and Mom is virtue signaling a lot, I think, in a kinda passive-aggressive and sanctimonious way. And they're always at Grandma and Grandpa's place, or used to be, and they do the same thing. I don't understand why we've almost never spent time at Dad's parents' place, they even live closer by. I just think that over the years, Dad has started to feel like an outlier."

"But that's no reason to cheat on someone?"

"I'm not saying it is. Dad shouldn't have done that. He should have talked to her about it, but you know what he's like. He doesn't have the language for that. Or he should have just left her and then he could have done whatever he wanted."

"So, *you're* not mad at Dad?" Jeremy's question leaves no question; *he's* certainly mad at their father.

"I am. But I guess I'm also mad at Mom. And I know I shouldn't be; you are supposed to be mad at the cheater, you're not supposed to be mad at the person who's been cheated on. But I can't help it." Gina notices that her brother looks at her, but she cannot tell whether it's an understanding glance or whether it's the opposite. "I don't know what I'm trying to say. Does it even make sense?"

"I think, I know what you mean," Jeremy says, trying to see it from her perspective: "Maybe you're just trying to add nuances to the whole villain-victim idea."

"Yeah, I guess you can put it like that." She pauses for a few seconds and then continues, "Do you solely see Mom as the victim and Dad as the villain?"

"Probably more than you do." Then it's his turn to pause for a few seconds before carrying on, "But let's not get too much into that."

"Exactly, it's their war, not ours. We don't wanna let this thing get between us." She's tearing up a bit, and her brother reaches across the table and takes her hand. "And I know I was giving Mom too much of a hard time the day she told us about the divorce. I should probably apologize someday, I even owe *you* an apology for that, I guess."

"Well, it's never too late to apologize to Mom. But don't worry about me. It's a closed chapter for me." He's holding both her hands now. "Mom was the only one you could react to, since Dad wasn't there. Like you said, you're mad at both of them. It would have been different if they had both been there to tell us."

"Perhaps you're right." Gina takes a deep breath before proceeding, "But I can't live with her. I'm sorry but I just can't." She looks at her twin brother and squeezes his hands, which haven't let go of hers, and sees that it's now his turn to have a lump in his throat. She knows him well enough to know that her decision doesn't come as a surprise to him, but she also knows him well enough to know that he has been hoping that she would have chosen otherwise.

She says, "Trust me, the last thing I wanted was for the two of us to stop living together because of *this*. I wanted us to move out on the same day, you know, hiring the same moving truck and all, and doing it because we were both ready to start a new chapter in our lives, I didn't want it to be like this. But I can't stay in this house."

"Do you hate Mom that much?" Jeremy says. He thought about saying that if she moves out of the house, their parents' war *does* become their war, and this thing *will* come between them and there will also be a river between the two of them, but decides not to. Gina has given him no reason to believe that it hasn't been a really tough decision for her, and there's no need to make it even more difficult for her. Instead, he says that he isn't trying to guilt-trip her with his question; he's just trying to understand her.

"I wouldn't put it like that. We've had our differences over the years, but of course I don't hate her."

"I know, I'm sorry. I didn't mean it like that," Jeremy explains.

"No worries. It also has a lot to do with Dad. If we both stay here, he becomes even more of a villain than he already is. I can't leave him hanging; I'm afraid he's gonna get lonely. He's not good at being on his own. Besides, I don't have to spend all my time there, I just want him to know that I'm living with *him*."

"You are a good daughter."

"Thanks. To *one* of my parents," Gina says with a shrug.

"Well, Mom gets to keep me, so I guess it all appears fair."

"So, you're not thinking about moving out anymore?"

"Not really. I did have a dorm room waiting, but I'm pretty sure I'm not gonna use it." Jeremy looks at his sister and suspects that she might not entirely approve of that decision. "But I don't mind staying here for one or two years. It makes it possible for me to save up some cash and perhaps I can buy my own place in a couple of years."

"But you've always wanted to live in a dorm?" Gina says.

"Things change."

"For you or for Mom?"

The second Gina asks that, Jeremy knows that his presumption was correct; she's not a fan of him staying at their mom's place, but since he knows that she has seen through him, he also knows that the best strategy now is to just level with her: "It's mainly for Mom's sake. Like I said, being able to save up money is fine, but you're right, if it hadn't been for the divorce I would've lit out of here right after the summer vacation."

"Fair enough."

"Is it?"

"I guess; you don't want Mom to be alone, I don't want Dad to be alone. I suppose there's some fairness to that." She considers encouraging him to live *his* life and is also close to saying that it's not really the same thing, because she wasn't planning on moving out. However, she realizes that nothing she says will change his mind, and voicing her opinion might change something between the two of them, so she remains silent and thus the some-fairness-to-that comment remains the last one.

After spending another hour in the kitchen, they retreat to the living room and decide to watch a movie. At first, it seems weird for Gina to be in the living room. It seems weird to even call it that—since there's obviously no *living* happening in there anymore—and she finds it peculiar that spending time in a room in which she has spent thousands of hours can give her an unpleasant feeling. Luckily, binge-watching *Stranger Things*, and falling asleep on and off while doing that, calms her nerves and at five o'clock they decide that it's time to get something to eat and after debating their options decide to get something that's better than your average fast food. An hour later, Gina picks up a Black Angus, flat iron steak and an oven roasted filet at Le Bouchon on 76 Main St., a restaurant which used to be her favorite when she was a kid, but now merely reminds her that she's not a kid any longer. When she returns to her car, she grabs her phone and notices that she has two missed calls from Jeremy and a snap that says: "Hurry home. Trump's been shot!"

Once back in the house, Gina rushes into the living room and finds the TV blaring; *Stranger Things* has been replaced by even stranger things and the expression "breaking news" does not even begin to describe the intensity with which every channel is covering the assassination attempt. Jeremy, who rarely swears, keeps whispering "He's been shot, he's been fucking shot," and his eyes are so glued to the screen that he barely registers that his sister is back or notices that she asks him if Trump is dead. Gina positions herself right beside him and puts her hands on his shoulders, not as a gesture of comfort, but just to let him know that she's there.

He mumbles something, but his words are redundant as MSNBC News has already shown her what she wanted to know: Donald Trump is incredulous, shocked, injured, wounded, lacerated, and bloodied but he's *alive*. He was less than an inch away from being killed, and now, instead, the pictures show a man who's more alive than he has ever been before; the defiantly raised fist, the unbowed look in his eyes, the blood on his face, the words that come out of his mouth as the agents evacuate him from the stage, words that are impossible to hear, but easy to lip read: "fight, fight, fight." At this exact point in time, Donald Trump comes across as the most invincible man on the face of the earth. And, on top of all this, there's the American flag in the background to complete the image of the immortal ex-president who's willing to take a bullet for his country.

Gina and Jeremy are speechless for the next two hours, as they learn that the shooter, Thomas Matthew Crooks, fired eight shots from the rooftop of a nearby building, slightly injuring the former president, hitting several people in the crowd, and killing a father who was trying to protect his family. Shortly after Crooks fired his own weapon, Secret Service snipers fired their weapons at him, which resulted in much more than just an injured ear and a bloodstained face; Crooks was killed only a few seconds after he thought *he* would be the killer, and the effect of his actions was likely the complete opposite of what he had intended. Instead of putting an end to Trump's dream of reentering the White House, the general consensus after the assassination attempt was that there was now no way that Biden could defeat Trump in the upcoming election. Even before Crooks' shoot-and-miss shots, Biden was trailing Trump in almost all polls, partly because Trump personified a strong man image, whereas Biden seemed exceedingly frail, lethargic, and old. This had always been the contrast between the two of them, but never before had the juxtaposition been so evident; whilst a madman with an AR-rifle couldn't kill Trump—he rose from the stage as if stung by nothing more than a bee—Biden was in his bed because of a mild case of coronavirus, and looked and sounded like a person who might never be able to leave that bed.

In addition, Gina and Jeremy also listened to commentators going on about how the assassination attempt would lead to a number of sympathy votes for Donald Trump. It was the first time that the twins were old enough to vote, and despite the fact that Gina had known for a while that she would cast her ballot for Trump, it could hardly be said that it was because she considered him sympathetic.

She, and many other others, considered him a lot of things; eccentric, energetic, outspoken, brash, patriotic, affirmative, assertive, forceful, decisive, vigorous, potent, commanding, insistent, strong-willed, but, as such, there was nothing sympathetic about Trump, and it was unlikely that unsympathetic leaders would get sympathy votes, *unless* they'd almost had their ear blown off by a madman with an AR rifle. An assassination attempt was bound to be one of the few things that could make people *sympathize* with Donald Trump. It was the perfect way for him to convince people that he was telling the truth when he said that the radical leftists were demonizing him and denouncing him as public enemy number one; a walking, talking threat to American society, who had to be stopped at all costs, even if that meant killing him. There was no mistaking the conclusion in the media coverage that played out in front of Gina and Jeremy as they sat glued to the TV screen for over three hours after Crooks fired his AR rifle; the bullets that failed to kill Trump killed Biden's political career instead; at nine o'clock at night, July 13, 2024, three hours after Trump was interrupted by the popping sounds of Crooks' weapon, no one in their right mind could imagine that Joe Biden could defeat Donald Trump in an election that was less than four months away.

"What a day," Gina says, indicating that she's ready to talk to her brother about the events that are unfolding in front of their eyes. Neither of them has said much for the past three hours, apart from the occasional "Oh my god" and "I can't believe this" accompanied by a lot of headshaking. "Can you believe this?"

"It's been one crazy day alright," Jeremy says. "I know there's a lot of anger out there, but I didn't expect something like this." Since he doesn't say anything about how lucky it was that Trump wasn't killed, Gina beats him to it.

"Good thing he wasn't killed." Jeremy remains quiet, so she continues, "I think all hell would've broken loose if he'd been killed."

"You're right about that," Jeremy says. However, it's uncertain whether he's referring to the first or the last thing his sister just said. This puzzles Gina, but she decides not to go into it and instead asks him about his assessment of the situation.

"Do you agree with all the smart people on TV? Do you think it's a given that he's gonna get elected now?"

"Yeah, they're probably right about that. Biden comes across as more and more weak, and Trump does the opposite. That's not gonna change."

Out of the blue, Gina starts to think about their father; she assumes that he's having a couple of beers while watching the coverage, and imagines how he got up from his seat when he saw the incident the first time, like a frenzied football fan who jumps from the couch when his favorite team is about to score a touchdown, and how it took a while before he regained his composure and sat back down. She knows that the only reason why he hasn't called is that he knows that she's with Jeremy, and he doesn't want to disturb them. However, since Gina knows that he would like to talk to someone, preferably her, about this, she texts him and lets him know that she'll call him soon. She then directs her attention to her brother again, and says, "Dad's gonna go crazy now."

"He sure is. And you?"

"Am I gonna go crazy?" Gina pretends that she doesn't understand the question.

"That's not exactly what I meant. But what do you think about all of this?"

"I'm not happy that Trump got shot, but I don't mind if he's re-elected; and if this helps his chances then I guess it's fine by me. What do you think?"

"I don't like the guy. I never did, and never will. I don't think he's fit to run this country. But there's not that much I can do about it. I can vote against him, but if he wins, so be it. At least, if he wins, he can only serve one more term, so it's four years down, four to go."

"But Biden's gonna be eighty-six when he retires as president, if he wins. Is that better?"

"He's too old, you are right about that, but anything's better than Trump, if you ask me. Just look at his reaction when he lost the election last time. Think about the "Stop the Steal"-speech and the Capitol Hill riots; people died for God's sake. The guy's a narcissistic lunatic, don't you think?"

"What I think is that we're starting to sound like Mom and Dad."

"You're right. Let's not go down that road."

"Speaking of our beloved parents, I promised Dad I would give him a call, so I'm gonna go do that."

"Good idea, I'll give Mom a call then."

As soon as Gina hears her father's voice, she knows that she was right about his reaction; he sounds tipsy and repeats the word "badass" a few times when he talks about Trump's reaction to the assassination attempt. They're on the phone for eight minutes and then Gina returns to the living room, where she's joined by her brother after twenty minutes. He apologizes for keeping her waiting that long— "You know what Mom is like"—but other than that doesn't mention anything about their talk, and Gina doesn't mention their father's repetition of the word badass. She just tells him that their Dad said hi, and he tells her that their mother did the same.

At ten o'clock they go into the kitchen and have dinner. Jeremy's Black Angus, flat iron steak is cold and so is Gina's oven roasted filet. Before going to bed, they smilingly agree upon the fact that they can hardly blame Le Bouchon for the cold dishes.

Chapter eight
Kamala Devi Harris

What I'm gonna do is fix the tax system. For example, we have a thousand trillionaires in America, I mean billionaires in America, and what's happening, they're in a situation, where they in fact pay 8.2 percent in taxes, if they just paid 24 percent, 25 percent, either one of those numbers, they'd raise five hundred million dollars, billion dollars, I should say, in a ten year period, we'd be able to wipe out his debt, we'd be able to help make sure that all those things we need to do, child care, elder care, making sure that we continue to supren...strengthen our healthcare system. Making sure that we're able to make every single solitary person, uh, uh, eligible for what I've been able to do with, with, with the COVID, uhm, excuse me, uhm, dealing with everything we have to do with...uh, look, uhhhhhh, if, we finally beat Medicare.

James plays the clip from the Biden-Trump TV debate one more time, and his wife, daughter, and grandson listen just as attentively the second time as they did the first time and reach the same conclusion: the president's words don't make sense; it's an old man speaking incoherently, while involuntarily mixing up his points about the tax system and Medicare.

Alicia's father then goes on about how Biden, despite his fifty-one years in politics, has never really been good at debating. He's decent enough when his teleprompter takes him through a speech, James explains, but Biden's debate performance, a little less than a month prior to this night, didn't surprise James that much; perhaps he hadn't expected Biden to perform that poorly, but he had feared that Donald Trump would come across as the stronger candidate.

James makes a point about being the only one around the table who's old enough to remember how a twenty-nine-year-old Biden, elected to the US senate for the first time in 1972, wasn't even good at debating when he was young, followed by the rhetorical question: How then, could an eighty-one-year-old Biden stand a chance in a debate against Donald Trump in 2024? "Sure, Biden has grown wiser, but what we mainly learned in CNN's Atlanta studio that June night," James says, "was that Biden's wisdom couldn't make up for the fact that his voice at times was so weak that it sounded more like the whisper of a hospital patient near the end than the voice of a US president hoping to be re-elected."

James then goes on to talk about how Biden also lapsed into confused silence at times during the debate, and while Trump spoke, the cameras occasionally showed pictures of Biden with his mouth gaping open, leaving the viewers with the impression of a president who was in every possible way past his prime; a weathered and timeworn man, who may have his heart in the right place, but who was far more synonymous with dementia and defeat than with vigor and victory. This was a boxer with his back against the ropes, but unfortunately there wasn't anybody in the corner who could throw in the towel, according to James, but, he continued, "Luckily this isn't just water under the bridge now, it's a blessing in disguise."

"Do you need to see the clip one more time?" James asks his grandson, because he has expressed his concern about whether or not their countrymen are ready to elect the first female president. And, Jeremy says, "a *Black-Indian* woman at that."

"No, I get it, Gramps. The Democrats didn't have a choice after Biden's performance at the debate, but I'm not sure that Kamala Harris is the right choice," Jeremy continues.

"Well, there's no such thing as a sure bet, so I'm not sure either, but I have a good feeling about it," James says and feels like a good grandfather who's trying to calm his grandson down.

Alicia and Jeremy hadn't come to her parents' house to talk about the sudden emergence of Vice President Kamala Harris in the presidential race, but to plan a getaway-weekend in New York for the four of them— Gina had somewhat politely turned down the invitation—but since the date is July 26, less than a week after Biden announced that he was raising the white flag, it was inevitable that the Democratic generational shift would be dissected by all four of them.

James continues, "It's only been five days, and it seems that people have already forgotten about her bad approval ratings. And there's just a huge difference between being Kamala Harris, the Vice President, who stands in the shadow of man who looks more like a shadow than a man, to being Kamala Harris, the Democratic nominee, who is within reach of becoming the first female President of the United States of America.

And when you add *her* race into the *presidential* race, you get the sort of thing that can create history; I think a lot of people are going to love the narrative of the Black-Indian *woman* who defeats Donald Trump."

"Enough people?" Jeremy, although smitten by his grandfather's optimism, looks skeptically at him.

"Hopefully so. Or perhaps I should say *probably* so. She has so much going for her, Jeremy." James knows that both his wife and daughter share his presidential prediction, so he now focuses almost exclusively on Jeremy during this conversation; it's the knowledgeable Nestor who passes not only his wisdom, but also his sanguinity, on to his concerned grandson. "There's also the whole prosecutor vs. the felon thing, which is gonna be such a good argument. Did you hear Harris the day after Biden passed the torch to her?"

James doesn't wait for an answer but grabs his phone, presses a few buttons and then reads aloud: "Before I was elected as vice president, I was a courtroom prosecutor. In those roles, I took on perpetrators of all kinds. Predators who abused women. Fraudsters who ripped off consumers. Cheaters who broke the rules for their own gain. So hear me when I say: I know Donald Trump's type." James looks up from the screen and nods approvingly at his grandson. "You see, she's turning this into a choice between the law enforcer vs. the law breaker. Trump has talked so much about being the law-and-order candidate, but he's now facing a candidate who doesn't have to stick to *talking* about law and order, she *is* law and order."

"Another thing is that it's now the Democrats who have the younger candidate," Alicia's mother says.

"The Republicans have talked so much about Biden's age in the past months, and now they're the ones with the old candidate. Obviously, Kamala Harris isn't young, but she's much younger than Trump."

James nods his head affirmatively towards his wife and lets everyone know that that is also a good point.

"And she represents *change*," Alicia says, as if also wanting to chime in and join forces with her parents in what appears to be a mission to assure Jeremy that everything will be alright; their favorite candidate will get elected. "Actually, I think she represents both change and sameness, because she, on the one hand, is a reflection of Biden's policies and achievements, which are decent enough, and on the other hand, she personifies something entirely different; one who can bring about change; she's the past and the future at the same time."

"And she's good on social media, isn't she, Jeremy?" Sharon asks, trying to make sure they also talk about things where *he's* the expert.

"I guess she is." Jeremy says. "I know that a lot of influencers and stars are lining up in support of her, and a lot of her TikTok memes are out there."

"She's getting a bit of a rockstar image on the internet, isn't she?" James asks.

"I guess you could say that. She also has something going with this pop star called Charlie XCX and an album of hers called *Brat*." Despite not entirely knowing what he's talking about, Jeremy can tell by the faces of her family members that he certainly knows more about it than them, so he offers a short elaboration: "I'm not entirely sure what it is, but it has something to do with this English singer, Charlie XCX, who tweeted 'Kamala IS Brat', which is a reference to her Sixth album. And then Kamala Harris just sort of embraced it and now a lot of young voters see her as the cool girl."

"Well, I'm not really sure I understand that, but I do understand that Trump probably wouldn't get away with something like that, so it sounds like a good thing," Sharon says. "And, like it or not, everything that happens on social media plays a role as well, and we'll take all the help we can get."

"You see, Jeremy, history was made when Biden posted this." James picks up a piece of paper and passes it on to his grandson. "A week ago, when I looked at Joe Biden, I thought to myself: as sure as the sun will rise, this man is going to lose this election." He points his finger at the paper and continues, "But now, the tables have turned."

Jeremy glances at the piece of paper and quickly realizes that it's a print-out of the post in which Biden announced that he was stepping down. He's not sure that he's ever really read the entire thing, so he spends the next two minutes doing that.

My Fellow Americans,

Over the past three and a half years, we have made great progress as a Nation.

Today, America has the strongest economy in the world. We've made historic investments in rebuilding our Nation, in lowering prescription drug costs for sen-

iors, and in expanding affordable health care to a record number of Americans. We've provided critically needed care to a million veterans exposed to toxic substances. Passed the first gun safety law in 30 years. Appointed the first African American woman to the Supreme Court. And passed the most significant climate legislation in the history of the world. America has never been better positioned to lead than we are today.

I know none of this could have been done without you, the American people. Together, we overcame a once-in-a-century pandemic and the worst economic crisis since the Great Depression. We've protected and preserved our Democracy. And we've revitalized and strengthened our alliances around the world.

It has been the greatest honor of my life to serve as your President. And while it has been my intention to seek reelection, I believe it is in the best interest of my party and the country for me to stand down and to focus solely on fulfilling my duties as President for the remainder of my term.

I will speak to the Nation later this week in more detail about my decision.

For now, let me express my deepest gratitude to all those who have worked so hard to see me reelected. I want to thank Vice President Kamala Harris for being an extraordinary partner in all this work. And let me express my heartfelt appreciation to the American people for the faith and trust you have placed in me.

I believe today what I always have: that there is nothing America can't do—when we do it together. We just have to remember we are the United States of America.

"Great, Gramps, that's just great." Jeremy says, and then James acknowledges Biden for doing the right and unselfish thing.

"Better late than never," Sharon says, before making it clear that she thinks Biden should have stepped down right after the debate. In fact, she even goes on to claim that he should've stuck to his original plan of being a one-term president, a statement which seems to fall on deaf ears.

Jeremy considers asking his grandfather why he has printed out Biden's post, but remembers that his grandfather can get superstitious from time to time and assumes that he has either done it because he thinks it might bring luck or because he just likes to have a piece of paper lying around to remind him that July 21 was the turning point for the nation; the day when Biden took the decision that ensured that his predecessor would not be his successor.

"So, can we eat now?" Jeremy asks. "We've established that Kamala Harris is gonna beat Donald Trump, and I'm starving now."

Fifteen minutes later, the food is on the table, and they're beginning to plan the New York getaway. Jeremy asks his mother if she's sure that Gina can't come, and she reassures him that she's already asked, and that Gina has declined.

He considers letting his mother know that she should do more to encourage Gina to go, but remains silent.

His grandfather doesn't say a word, nor does his grandmother—except for commenting on how delicious the food is.

*

Meanwhile, not too far away from James and Sharon's house, Gina is hanging out with her father at the auto shop. She'd told herself that she wouldn't spend too much time there, let alone spend the night there, but when she pictures Jeremy, Alicia, James, and Sharon together, she feels an overwhelming urge to be with her father. It's not because Johnny knows that the rest of the family is dining together. Gina could go there without him finding out, and she could even join them on the New York getaway without him finding out, and even if he were to find out he wouldn't bat an eye. Yet something inside her prompts her not to put him in this situation where five people gather for a nice meal around the dining table in the comforts of an oversized house, while he's spending the night by himself in an ergonomic chair in an undersized office. So, despite the hassle of having to bring her stuff to his office, and the inconvenience of having to go from the office to her work in the morning, and despite the discomforting back pain that comes from sleeping on the office mattrass, this is now the third night in the past three weeks when Smith's Carmarket is her home for the night.

It's seven o'clock at night when Johnny lets his daughter know that he has finally closed up the store and they go get take away at the local Chipotle. Once back at the office, they turn the office desk into something that resembles a dining table and consume their meal with the TV blaring in the background. They're not watching the TV as such, but since a TV in the background can rarely be completely ignored, it's impossible for them not to devour their burritos while hearing about the changing dynamics of the presidential election race. From the moment they turn on the TV to the moment they turn it off, everything is about Kamala Harris. Kamala this, Kamala that. Kamala, Kamala, Kamala. A little past nine o'clock, Johnny has had enough, turns off the TV, and tells his daughter that she has nothing to worry about because this Black-Indian woman isn't going to win the election since no one knows who she is or what she stands for.

In the days and weeks after Biden passed the torch to Kamala Harris, Gina works extra shifts at the café, which is exhausting but also provides a temporary escape from some of her worries. At no point does she regret the decision to move in with her dad, but as their moving day approaches, a list of concerns builds up inside her mind; she worries about moving further away from Liam; she doesn't like to see her father drink and has recently brooded over the fact that divorced-Johnny seems to drink even more than married-Johnny; she knows that it will be difficult for her dad to make ends meet and would like to chip in but that would prolong the process of saving up enough money to eventually get her own place; she will only see her brother about once a week, and her mother even less than that and is also worried that she will lose touch with her neighborhood friends.

Other misgivings about their new place concern the number of square feet. Initially, Gina was mainly worried about how her father would react to the involuntary downsizing, but it's beginning to dawn on her that the domestic shrinking applies to her as well. She isn't a girly girl who needs the bathroom for a long time for her morning routine. However, she still figures that having to live in a place with only one bathroom—for the first time in her life since they moved out of the Park Slope apartment when she was a toddler and spent most of her time at home naked and without worries about seeing her parents undressed—is far from optimal.

Likewise, they're moving into a one-bedroom apartment so either she gets a bedroom or her dad does, and she doesn't know which solution she prefers. Lastly, Gina worries about the fact that, initially, the main reason for moving in with her dad was to prevent him from getting lonely, but she now contemplates the idea that he can be lonely for a long time, possibly even a longer time than she wants to live there. Thus, before even moving in, she's beginning to worry about when she can move out. When the speculations overwhelm Gina, she shakes her head and taps her cheeks a couple of times until she can once again convince herself that things won't be so bad after all.

In between all the extra shifts at work, and all the concerns as to whether moving in with her father is the right thing to do, Gina finds only a little time to pay attention to the news, and since her boyfriend is only moderately interested in politics and rarely brings up the presidential race, the "Kamalamania" which builds up in the weeks following Biden's announcement of his stepping down goes more or less unnoticed. It's hardly a lack of interest that causes her lack of attention to this; she just seems incapable of wrapping her head around it right now. When Gina is with Liam, and they do find themselves watching the news, they usually only spend a few minutes doing this, until one of them puts their hand inside the other one's pants and they give into their youthful impulses.

Her father, however, finds it difficult not to pay close attention to what the media, much to his vexation, calls the "rise of Kamala Harris". He considers it very premature to talk about a *rise*; he cannot see how she has earned her position as the Democratic nominee; had it not been for the further withering of her already-withered boss she would still be running for vice-president, and she certainly hasn't won anything yet. In those waning days of July, Johnny convinces himself that Harris isn't a threat to Trump. This is despite having to admit that the Democratic Party did seem to enjoy an explosion of enthusiasm, and in spite of having to turn off the TV on more than one occasion because it worries him to hear about endorsements across the party and it annoys him to hear about how the Democratic Party raised eighty-one million dollars in twenty-four hours and persuaded tens of thousands of volunteers to join their campaign. Despite all the other good stories that are relayed from the Democratic campaign these days, he's still certain that none of it will matter on election day.

Likewise, Johnny doesn't enjoy hearing about it when Harris officially makes Tim Walz her running mate for the White House; he has to give it to the Democrats—this is probably a good pick. Walz is everything Harris is not; he's a regular, plain, and blunt guy who can hardly be associated with the technocratic coastal elites and his denouncing of Trump and Vance as *weird* is a bull's-eye comment—as much as it bothers Johnny to admit that. And then, of course, Walz is white, so he and Harris complement each perfectly in this context, and although Johnny would argue that Walz is white in an almost bland way, it is difficult to argue against the fact that Walz comes across as a what-you-see-is-what-you-get guy, making him as trustworthy and relatable as they come. At the end of the day, Johnny does have to admit that if it wasn't for the fact that Walz was running to become Harris' vice president, this would be the sort of guy he wouldn't mind having a couple of beers with, and the same can't be said about either Donald Trump or JD Vance.

However, the fact of the matter is that Walz *is* Harris' running mate, and, as such, a political enemy, who might reduce Trump's chances of returning to the White House, and whenever Johnny hears enough from or about Walz he does what has by now become his preferred strategy: he turns off the TV and reminds himself that the "Kamalamania" movement is losing its momentum.

On a sunny August morning, Gina and her dad have both taken a day off work and begin the process of hauling all their belongings into a moving truck. Since their stuff is located in three different places, including the office at Smith's Carmarket, Liam's house, and what used to be their house in Cold Spring, it is a lengthy procedure and it's not until late in the afternoon, August 18, that they unlock the door to their new apartment and begin un-hauling boxes, bags, electronics, rugs, lamps, and pillows. After two hours of hard work, only two things need to be carried into the apartment: a couch that folds out as a bed and an actual bed.

Afterwards, they enjoy their Taco Bell takeout on the couch and make a list of all the items that are still needed before their new place can actually be called a home. Shortly after, Gina goes to bed, partly because she's exhausted from all the moving, but also because she has to get up early the next morning as she and Liam have taken a few days off work and have planned a Boston get-away. She thinks it will be nice for her father to have the new place to himself the first few days, allowing him to get settled in his own way and in his tempo.

Johnny has told his dad that he won't be in the auto shop the next three days, which should give him plenty of time to get settled. The days off work also enable him to reach for the bottle and for the pack of cigarettes, and as soon as he detects that Gina is sound asleep in the bedroom he pops open his first beer and chugs it down in less than five minutes. He prolongs the enjoyment of the next beer a bit—it takes almost ten minutes to knock that one back—and as he opens his third beer, he becomes aware of the fact that although Gina might leave the apartment early next morning, she will still notice how many beers he has had. If he leaves the empty beer bottles somewhere in the apartment, she'll notice them, and if he removes them from the apartment and takes them down to the trash cans, she'll still think about the fact that there were six beers in the fridge when she went to bed, and the next morning there were only three. Johnny doesn't mind his daughter knowing that he's had three beers, but suspects that she'll be worried if she finds out that he's had more, and although thinking that she's overly sensitive when it comes to his alcohol intake, he decides to stick to three beers and instead pours himself a glass of Glenfiddich afterwards.

When he has enjoyed two glasses of *ol'Glen* he starts wondering if Gina would be observant enough to notice how much whiskey has disappeared over the night, and though telling himself that she likely won't, he pours a glass of water into the whiskey bottle before leaving the apartment and walking all the way down to the trash station with four cigarette stubs. Once back in the apartment, he opens all windows in the living room and collapses on the couch, without folding it out as a bed, since he simply doesn't have the energy to do that.

Four hours later, Johnny registers the sound of his daughter having breakfast but decides to pretend that he's asleep—an act which he keeps up for the next forty-five minutes while she's showering and then packing her stuff. It's not until after she's left the apartment that he staggers into the bathroom for his morning piss and a couple of ibuprofen pills, whereupon he returns to the couch, turns on the TV, and goes back to sleep.

When Johnny wakes up several hours later, the TV immediately reminds him that the Democratic National Convention has begun and while this is not in any way his preferred method of being brought back to his senses, it's not terribly frustrating to hear that Biden will give his speech later that night; he might even consider watching it.

However, when he learns that Hillary Clinton will probably step onto the stage in less than an hour, he immediately turns off the TV. His stomach is upset, though not to the point where he has to throw up, so he takes a shower and starts unpacking his stuff. Following this, he spends an hour familiarizing himself with the apartment; he locates the circuit breaker, finds the water shutoff valve, and tests the smoke detectors. Then he texts Gina and lets her know that he will explore the neighborhood; he intends to find the nearest grocery store and the local pharmacy and will also be looking for local amenities like parks, coffee shops, and a gym.

When Johnny leaves his apartment, he walks right into his neighbor, a middle-aged woman, who introduces herself as Janet. She's good-looking, but probably not out of his league, although he's no longer sure what his league is. He introduces himself and tells her that he just moved in last night, but apart from that he doesn't really know what to say and ends up awkwardly excusing himself because he's late for a meeting.

As he leaves the parking lot, he feels slow-witted in a way that he hasn't since his teenage years. He has thought about the absurdity of the fact that he so regularly had sex when he was married, occasionally even with his wife, but now that he's divorced and doesn't have to bother with the sneaking around and the feeling of shame—however tiny that feeling may have been—he hasn't had sex at all. It's been three and a half months since his cock was inside a woman, and ever since he pulled it out of that Manchester girl's pussy, the sole purpose of his male organ, apart from a few morning showers during which he has masturbated, has been letting the urine leave his bladder and his body. Apart from female customers at Smith's Carmarket, female waiters and cashiers, and an angry ex-wife, Janet is the only woman he has had a word with since that life-changing weekend trip to New York in early April. In order for Johnny to carry on with his day, he convinces himself that he just got caught on the wrong foot; chatting up women has always been his thing, and still is, and as soon as he decides that he's ready to throw himself into the dating game, his dick will no longer be missing in action; he even convinces himself that Janet might be the first woman who can be swayed by post-divorce Johnny, and on that note continues with his day. Returning to the apartment, he has another evening of three beers and plenty of whiskey. Shortly after midnight, he crawls onto the couch and masturbates while picturing himself doing Janet from behind.

The morning after, Johnny feels much less hungover than the day before and after breakfast immediately gets started; he has several shelves to put on the walls and has promised Gina that there will be a mirror on one of the walls in the bedroom when she returns from their Boston get-away. He also has to install two light fixtures in the living room and one in the bedroom and he's hoping that he can unpack the last of his stuff. After working ceaselessly for almost eight hours, he allows himself the pleasure of today's first beer and, turning on the TV, reminds himself that today is the day when the Obamas will be speaking at the DNC.

Just as his microwave dinner is ready, Michelle Obama takes the stage and for reasons unknown to himself, Johnny doesn't turn off the TV. Initially, he's listening to her, then his focus switches from listening to watching, and eventually he finds himself imagining what his dick would look like in her mouth. He considers jacking off again, and although his fatigue prevents him from beginning, he's left with an invigorating feeling; his bodily impulses are starting to make him feel like a man again. He smells sex; Michelle Obama is a fantasy of course but his neighbor is not.

When one Obama passes the microphone to the next Obama, Johnny once again finds himself reluctant to turn off the TV and ends up sitting through the entirety of Barack Obama's thirty-five minutes on stage and even ends up admitting that he pulls off a good performance. Obama's suggestion that Trump's fixation on crowd sizes possibly reflects an insecurity about the size of his penis makes the audience go crazy and even Johnny cannot help finding the comment a bit amusing. Similarly, he acknowledges that Obama's brain works not only impeccably but also rapidly, when the former President hears someone in the crowd shouting out his former presidential slogan, "Yes we can," which he instantly turns into the phrase, "Yes she can."

Listening to Obama doesn't bother Johnny as much as he had imagined, but once he opens his second beer, he starts imagining how Alicia and her parents are gathered around the TV to celebrate how energized the Democratic Party has become after Kamala Harris has provided political resuscitation to her and her boss's project. He imagines how his former father-in-law repeats the word "energized" and since he likes to come across as a walking-talking thesaurus, Johnny supposes that he goes on to use words such as "invigorated", "revitalized", "rejuvenated", and "stimulated" when explaining just how excited he is about the turn of events in the presidential race and how sure he is that Kamala Harris will remain a resident of 1600 Pennsylvania Avenue even after January 20.

Johnny goes on to picture how they will all meet again Thursday, when Kamala Harris gives her acceptance speech and James will sit down beside his grandson and wrap his arm around his shoulder, telling him some Democratic bullshit about how they are watching history in the making. He'll tell Jeremy to look at all the Democratic banners and signs and he will cheer loudly as thousands and thousands of Democratic ballons drop from the roof at the conclusion of the DNC. He might even have filled up their own living-room with Democratic ballons, and everything will be so demo-fucking-cratic that it almost makes Johnny sick to his stomach, and he figures that the best cure for that is one more beer but, since that doesn't work, he convinces himself that a Jack Daniels and coke is the best cure, and since that does seem to work—he eventually forgets about his political missionary of a former father-in-law—he finishes the bottle, which amounts to exactly five more drinks.

The morning after, Johnny is hungover and again finds himself conjuring up images of how Alicia's father uses the DNC to convince Jeremy that Harris is undoubtedly ready to become the next president. Johnny envisions how James argues that Harris has enough political experience to take "the next, big step"; she was a district attorney, an attorney general, a US Senator, and is now the Vice President. The more that conversation, which is closer to a monologue, plays out in Johnny's head, the more he considers opening a beer, but since it's not even noon, he decides on a different plan; rather than suffering the exasperation of imagining Jeremy cuddled up between his mother and her parents during Kamala Harris' speech, he decides to call him and invite him over for dinner tomorrow night. Johnny knows that he can't convince Jeremy not to vote for Harris—he's much too influenced by his mother for that to be even remotely possible—but it's possible that he can cook a nice meal for them and the DNC can provide a backdrop for the evening and, if nothing else, then at least his son gets to see where his dad lives.

Jeremy sounds somewhat surprised when he picks up the phone, but he also lets his father know that he's glad he called and he appreciates the invitation; however, he politely has to decline, as he has promised his mother to have dinner with her parents. Johnny tries to find comfort in telling himself that at least he tried, and at least he has reached out to his son very shortly after he has moved into his new apartment, and luckily Jeremy did say that he would love to stop by the following weekend.

Nonetheless, Johnny's frustrations are not entirely gone and while he is, once again, tempted to turn to liquor, he manages to adhere to his newfound principle of not consuming alcohol before noon and instead lays down on the couch again and goes back to sleep.

The dial tone from Johnny's iPhone wakes him up a couple of hours later when Gina calls and lets him know that she's on her way home. They weren't supposed to return until the day after but have decided to cut the trip short and will be in the apartment in less than four hours, which forces Johnny to get up from the couch, since he knows that he needs to tidy the place before his daughter gets back. He begins by removing all the empty beer and liquor bottles, then he gathers all the cigarette stubs before opening all the windows and letting fresh air replace the apartment's *I have been drinking and smoking and not showered for the last three days* air. He then begins doing dishes and, since it's the first time he does that in his new apartment, there's a whole pile of plates, forks and knives, some of which have stains that are completely dried and caked on from sitting unwashed for so long. What would have otherwise been a ten-minute task ends up taking half an hour. Luckily for Johnny, he doesn't have to spend time on the foldable couch, as he still hasn't bothered to unfold it and turn it into a bed, so he can go straight to vacuuming the living room and, upon completing that task, the apartment looks more or less presentable, and he even has time to catch an hour's sleep before his daughter gets there.

At exactly six o'clock, Liam and Gina enter the apartment, and they gather around the table and start eating the takeout that they have brought. Johnny is glad to see his daughter again and also appreciates that Liam has joined them tonight, because he wants to see his girlfriend's new place. They enthusiastically tell him about everything they did in Boston, and Johnny pretends to listen but is really just considering whether or not he should give in to the almost irresistible urge to grab a beer. When he finally surrenders to the urge, he soon realizes that the beer makes it way easier for him to focus on their stories, and when he gets a second beer his hangover starts to disappear and he loosens up to the point where he tells them about his first few days in the apartment, and suddenly they have spent three hours around the table and Gina asks her father and her boyfriend if they want to watch Harris' acceptance speech. When they nod yes, she quickly removes all the trash from the table and shortly after they are on the couch, which makes it a bit easier for Johnny to accept the fact that twenty miles from here his son and ex-wife are bundled together at his former parents-in-law's house. Although Harris rubs him the wrong way from the beginning of the speech, and although he whispers "not to me" when she says "I promise to be a president for all Americans", he's still enjoying the moment; he's on his third beer, he doesn't feel lonely, he knows that his daughter is going to vote for Trump, and feels confident that Liam will do the same, though he hasn't specifically stated that, and there's something about the situation that makes him think that things will be alright.

Chapter nine
They're eating the dogs

It's a lovely September night and Alicia and Jeremy have just finished eating and are now getting ready to watch the presidential debate. They have just learned that this marks the first time that the two candidates will meet each other in real life, and as Jeremy leaves the kitchen, his mother finds herself wondering whether Harris will be intimidated by Trump's stage presence. Twenty seconds later, she calls her son's name and tells him to hurry as the debate is about to begin. When Jeremy enters the living room again, he concludes that he hasn't missed anything, since he hears Linsey Davis, the ABC anchorwoman who hosts the debate alongside David Muir, telling the viewers that it's almost showtime: "Good evening, we are looking forward to a spirited and thoughtful debate." However, Alicia lets her son know that he did miss something: "You should have seen the handshake," she says. "She strode across the debate stage, offered her hand to him, and introduced herself. She seems very confident, almost as if she's gonna hunt him down tonight," and even before the actual debate begins, Alicia tells herself that she has nothing to worry about; Harris is definitely not intimidated by her opponent.

"Interesting," Jeremy says. "What was his reaction?"

"He seemed a bit surprised, and you certainly got the impression that he hadn't planned on shaking her hand. And then I think he said, 'Nice to see you, have fun.'" Alicia then stops talking because the candidates start talking. Alicia and Jeremy zero in on the TV as the first topic, the economy, is presented. The rules of the debate have already been established: Harris is given two minutes to initiate the deliberation and, following this, Trump is given two minutes for his first rebuttal. Muir and Davies have also explained that the two candidates cannot interrupt each other as their microphones are turned off while the other candidate is talking.

During Trump's first comment of the night, Alicia lets her son know that the former president is mixing apples and oranges: "It didn't take long for him to turn the attention to the issue of immigration; we're not even two minutes into his first comment about the economy, and he's already talking about immigrants in Springfield and Aurora."

"Grandpa said his campaign advisors have probably told him to do that; the more he can turn the attention to the issue of immigration, the better," Jeremy says.

"Well, he's right about that. But it's also seen as an advantage for Trump to talk about the economy."

"Okay, you're probably right then; he's confusing the two topics."

"As he is with everything else," Alicia says, before David Muir lets Trump know "that we will get to immigration later tonight". Alicia and Jeremy acknowledge the fact that the host moderated Trump so early in the debate, and then they rejoice in the fact that they were right about their theory—Trump did begin the debate by mixing two matters—and they keep doing that so much that they don't even hear the part where Trump explains himself by saying that "bad immigration leads to bad economy" and suddenly they notice that the debate has turned to the issue of abortion.

"This is probably the one topic where she really has the upper hand," Jeremy says. His mother only briefly comments on that but he can tell that she likes what she's hearing before Harris even begins to speak. This time Trump gets the opening statement, and Alicia sits back with a satisfied look on her face as he goes on about how a lot of Democrats are in favor of abortions in the ninth month, and the look on her face becomes increasingly triumphant as Trump goes on to mention how some Democrats are even in favor of executing babies after birth. Alicia knows that this will be debunked by the moderator as soon as he stops talking, and as soon as Linsey Davis has done just that, Alicia knows that it will be easy for Harris to score points now.

"You really need to pay attention now, Jeremy," Alicia says. "She's gonna use all her rhetoric skills at this point to prove that she has the upper hand on this." She smiles victoriously as Harris goes on to refer to the woman who was told by Oklahoma hospital staffers that she had to wait in her car until she became sick enough to qualify for an abortion under the state's near-total ban. The staff agreed that she had a potentially life-threatening pregnancy complication but didn't believe they could legally treat her.

At no point does Harris mention Jaci Statton's name; instead, she uses her as an example to clarify that a post-Roe America is not what most people want: "She's bleeding out in the car in the parking lot. She didn't want that. Her husband didn't want that. A twelve- or thirteen-year-old survivor of incest being forced to carry a pregnancy to term? They don't want that." Alicia is almost clapping her hands as she lets her son know how well she thinks Harris handles this part of the debate.

A commercial break allows both Jeremy and Alicia to stretch their legs but once seated on the couch again, they are both immediately on pins and needles as David Muir introduces the next topic, which is immigration, and their hearts skip a beat as he points out that "Harris was tasked by Biden to get to the root causes of migration from Central America".

The split screen shows the face of a somewhat nervous Harris when Muir introduces the matter. It is obvious that she really keeps her ear to the ground, as the host reminds Harris and the millions of people who are watching the debate that "Illegal border crossings reached a record high in the Biden Administration". While Muir goes on to point out that these numbers have dropped significantly since then because of tougher asylum restrictions, he also rounds off his introduction of the issue by questioning why the Biden Administration waited until six months before the election to act on the situation at the border.

"This might be a tough question for her to answer," Jeremy mumbles, and before his mother can even begin to answer, they notice how Harris calls attention to the fact that there was a plan to bring 1,500 more agents to the border but also emphasizes that Trump got on the phone and called people in Congress and told them to kill the bill, because he would "prefer to run on a problem, instead of fixing a problem" and they agree that this is seemingly a good way of dodging the question.

Next, they observe how Harris moves on to address Trump's rallies by inviting the viewers to attend one of these so that they can see for themselves how people are leaving his rallies out of boredom and exhaustion.

"Is she doing this to provoke him?" Jeremy asks.

"She probably is. She´s probably trying to piss him off and get him to say something farfetched about the issue, so that this theme doesn't end up working as an advantage for him after all; we'll see what comes next."

"If he comments on the thing about his rallies, he's walking right into her trap, wouldn't you say?"

"Definitely—" and before she gets to continue the sentence, it's evident to both of them that Trump does walk headfirst into that trap; he begins his rebuttal by talking about the magnitude of his rallies and claiming that people don't go to Harris' rallies, and those who do are paid to go there.

Alicia and Jeremy smilingly look at each other and raise their hands in triumph, knowing that this couldn't possibly be any better. Harris and Trump are on the issue of immigration and he's not even talking about immigration.

She's teasing him and exposing him for the megalomanic man he is, and before they know it, and before they have even lowered their hands again, the situation gets even better for them, as Trump now does begin to address the actual issue, but in a way that they both instinctively know, despite being only halfway through the debate, will go down as the most memorable moment of the entire evening:

"IN SPRINGFIELD, THEY'RE EATING THE DOGS," Trump wails.

"THE PEOPLE THAT CAME IN, THEY'RE EATING THE CATS," he continues.

"THEY'RE EATING THE PETS OF THE PEOPLE THAT LIVE THERE," he rounds off.

They both savor the moment when one side of the split screen shows Trump saying these things with steam coming out of his ears, while the other side shows Harris laughing. "Her laugh shows that she got exactly what she wanted," Alicia says.

"This makes him look even dumber than he is."

"Certainly. He could have talked about the fact that Springfield has a population of roughly sixty thousand people and how twenty thousand immigrants have moved to the city in recent years. It would have been fair enough to bring attention to any challenges which might come from that."

"He could have. But it's cats and dogs. I can't wait to see the memes and stuff that will come out of this," Jeremy says, and then they chuckle and exchange high-fives as David Muir has once again fact-checked Trump and lets him know that they "did reach out to the city manager there and he told us there have been no credible reports or specific claims of pets being harmed, injured or abused by individuals within the immigrant community". Both Jeremy and Alicia think that the debate has taken an absurd turn, and that Harris handles this to perfection when it is once again her turn to speak, as she simply states, "Well, talk about extreme."

The rest of the debate passes without any memorable moments, or at least any moments that are as memorable as Trump's comment about animal-eating-immigrants, and when the two candidates round off there is no doubt in Alica or Jeremy's opinion that Harris wiped the floor with Trump and she's one step closer to the White House. In fact, they go on to ask themselves how anyone can even consider voting for Donald Trump, but then they remember that going too far down that road is also an insult to their father/ex-husband and their son/brother, so instead they start talking about the fact that they haven't seen the apartment that Gina and Johnny have moved into.

"I think I'll go there later this weekend," Jeremy says, and pauses before continuing the sentence, as he wants to see if his mother shows any reaction to that. "They've lived there for almost a month now, and I promised Gina that I wouldn't wait too long before visiting her." There's a moment of silence before he changes his own sentence: "Before visiting them."

"That sounds like a good plan," his mother says. "It's been more than a week since I spoke to Gina—how is she?"

"She's doing alright. It's a tiny place, but she says that they've settled into a good routine."

"Has she said anything about his drinking?"

"Not really. I don't think it's been a problem. It's not something she's mentioned."

"Good. I hope that he doesn't drink too much when she's there. I just hope that it all works out for her there."

"We could go and check for ourselves."

"You mean that *we* go and visit *them*."

"Yes. Being in this house is difficult for Gina, so you might need to go there if you want to see her. At least for the time being." Jeremy looks his mother in her eyes before carrying on. "But I know it's difficult for you."

"It is. But I have to make up my mind; what is more important to me? Seeing her or not seeing him?"

"I guess you can put it like that. Are you ready for it?"

"No, but I don't think I'll ever be."

"And you can't postpone it much longer!"

"What do you mean?"

"Well, what about Christmas for instance?"

Alicia considers a snappy comeback—*Well, what about Christmas?*—or something similar to that, but reminds herself that it wouldn't be fair to her son. Though he's an adult, in this case he's just a kid who's adjusting to this new-normal life but still occasionally reminisces about their old life, and wishes that his parents can celebrate Christmas together and, if nothing else, then at least pretend that things are the same as they used to be. Instead, she tells him that she still hasn't thought about those December nights, which is true, but says that she would like it if the four of them could get together for Christmas, which is a statement that is really something in between an exaggeration and a downright lie.

"So, what do you think?" Jeremy looks at her mother with eyes glowing with hope and optimism. Surely, her not ruling out the possibility of the four of them getting together for Christmas has lifted his spirit.

The look in his eyes reminds her of when he was a kid asking for a very specific gift for Christmas, and something inside of Alicia makes her want to give him that gift.

"What do I think about what? Christmas?"

"No, what do you think about the two of us visiting the two of them relatively soon? I could call Gina and ask her if we could stop by Saturday."

"It's not a bad idea."

"Mom, what does that mean?"

"It means go ahead and do it; I have a few days to wrap my head around it. I'll be fine." Alicia is on the threshold of tears as the words leave her mouth, and since it's too difficult for her to hide the fact that her heart is skipping several beats, she retreats to the bathroom and allows a few tears to roll down her cheeks.

However, she knows that Jeremy will sense that something is going on if she spends too much time in there, so she does her best to snap out of it, and moves to the kitchen where she buys herself two more minutes by making a cup of tea. Reentering the living room, she asks her son if he wants a cup as well. She's somewhat relieved when he declines and instead tells her how tired he is. Once he has retired to his room, Alicia turns the TV off and stares at a blank wall for a couple of hours; the last thing she does before going to bed is pour her full cup of tea into the kitchen sink.

*

Gina and her dad are having their morning coffee while discussing last night's debate and agreeing that Trump was ultimately the better candidate. They complain a bit about the fact that Harris was hardly factchecked at all, whereas they constantly seemed to run a check on things said by *their* candidate. They-are-eating-the-pets memes and YouTube clips have already gone viral and, while they do acknowledge some sort of absurdity in those Trump statements, it's not really something that they dwell on. "That's just Trump being Trump," Johnny says. "At least he cares about immigration," he continues, as Gina puts her cup down and says she has to get ready for school.

Normally, Johnny would ignore the dial tone from Gina's iPhone since he's gotten used to living with a teenager. He knows her phone is ringing, buzzing, vibrating, beeping, and chiming repeatedly from the moment she opens her eyes to the moment she closes them. "Your little machine has gone haywire again," he sometimes tells his daughter, but he's usually able to take no notice of her phone as it is usually in her pocket, in her right hand, or at least very close to her. This morning, however, Gina leaves her phone as she gets up from her seat, and it's now sitting on the kitchen table, right in front of his eyes, and, as he looks at the screen, which almost illuminates his face with the light that glows from the little device, he sees his son's name in the display. For a brief moment, Johnny thinks that it would be weird if he answered the call but then concludes that it would be even weirder if he didn't.

"Hey, son," Johnny says and remains quiet for a couple of seconds to give Jeremy time to respond. However, Jeremy doesn't say anything, so Johnny continues. "Gina's just gone to the bathroom, and she left her phone at the table, and when I saw your name in the display, I figured I'd just pick it up."

"No worries, Dad. I just had something I wanted to ask her, but I can talk to you about it."

"I'm all ears."

"Well, I still haven't seen your new place, so we talked about stopping by this weekend."

"That's a great idea. When do you wanna come?"

"We talked about Saturday afternoon, if you guys don't have any plans?"

"Oh, so you already talked to Gina about it?"

"No, not yet. That's why I'm calling."

"So, who is *we*? You and Mom?"

"That would be Mom and me, yes." Jeremy knows that his father didn't expect this and is anxious to hear the answer; he realizes that going there will be difficult for his mother but hasn't thought that it might be difficult for his father as well.

"I see." Johnny sounds just as surprised as Jeremy expected. "That sounds nice, you're more than welcome," he continues, and his son doesn't detect anything in his tone that suggests that he doesn't mean it.

"Great. Is Saturday alright?"

"Saturday is fine by me. I don't have any plans, and I don't think Gina has either. She's still in the shower, but do you need to talk to her as well?"

"No, that's alright, I'll talk to her later. See you Saturday afternoon, Dad."

"See you, son. I look forward to seeing you."

Though he should start getting ready for work, Johnny stays in his seat for another fifteen minutes after the conversation has come to an end. When Gina returns to the kitchen, he immediately asks if she has any plans for Saturday afternoon, and when she says that she doesn't, he tells her that she does now, as her brother and mother will be stopping by. Gina's jaw almost hits the floor when she hears this, but her father senses a smile hidden somewhere beneath her surprised look.

"Have you spoken to Jeremy?" Gina asks.

"Yes, I spoke to him, while you were in the shower."

"Did he call you?"

"Well, technically he called *you*, but your phone was right in front of me, so I just answered his call."

"How do you feel about that?"

"Fine. I'm glad that Jeremy wants to stop by. I've been meaning to invite him, but haven't gotten around to it, so it's nice that he beat me to it and reached out."

"And Mom?"

"I'd be lying if I said I wasn't surprised that she's coming as well, but it's fine by me. You guys deserve parents who have buried the hatchet and can spend time together with their kids. But I didn't think it would happen this soon."

"Is that why she's coming? Do you think she has buried the hatchet?" Gina gives her father an aren't-you-just-pushing-your-luck look.

"You may be right. Maybe she hasn't buried the hatchet, but it appears she hasn't sharpened it either."

"You're probably right. Maybe we'll be one big happy family on Saturday afternoon."

"Well, hopefully we can have a decent time." Johnny knows that his daughter's last comment is frustration disguised as humor, and though none of them are inclined to talk about feelings, he decides that now would be a good time. "Are you okay with it?"

"Am I okay with what? Mom stopping by Saturday or this newfound living situation of ours?"

"We can talk about either one of those things, sweetheart."

"It's alright that Mom's stopping by," Gina says and then, looking at her father, she realizes that she has to continue. "As for the other thing, let's talk about that when I'm not on my way out the door."

"Sure thing, sweetheart. Have a nice day at school."

They've lived in the apartment for three weeks now, but Gina was out of town the first few days and after that they have been busy settling in and adjusting, and Johnny hasn't had the time or the courage to ask Gina how she feels about living with him. Thus, he's glad that he has now given her the opportunity to express herself, but at the same time he's relieved because he knows that she might not necessarily use that opportunity. Five minutes later, when the events of this Wednesday morning have sunk in, he gets ready for work.

As Johnny leaves his apartment, he checks himself in the mirror and arrives at the conclusion that he's finally beginning to look like his old self. He's been contemplating this idea for the past couple of weeks; shortly after moving into the apartment he was annoyed by the scruffy look and the beer belly that were staring back at him in the mirror, and since then he has improved his skincare routine, had a haircut, improved his diet, and worked out regularly, and while he still drinks whenever he can get away with it, living with Gina simply offers fewer opportunities for drinking than does living by himself in the office, so he sometimes goes two or three days without alcohol.

As such, it's a solidly confident Johnny Roy Smith who leaves his apartment this bright morning; a man, who, despite not having had sex for the past five months, feels sexually attractive and is convinced that most women will see him the same way, and therefore, when he meets Janet, doesn't miss out on the opportunity of complimenting her good looks, and thereafter convinces himself that since that is the seventh time he has flirted with her since their first meeting, he'll invite her in for a cup of coffee next time he talks to her.

Come Saturday afternoon, when Jeremy and Alicia pull up to the apartment complex, they talk about the fact that it's odd that they have lived so close to this place for so many years, yet this is their first time there. They also ponder the fact that for Jeremy it has been almost two weeks since he has seen his sister and almost two months since he has seen his father, and for Alicia it has been a little more than a month since she has seen her daughter and roughly four months since she has seen her ex-husband, whom she otherwise, apart from the seventy-two weekend trips during which he cheated on her, or attempted to, has been used to seeing more or less every single day for the past twenty years. Both of them feel a bit on edge as Alicia turns off the engine and the fading music from the car radio leaves them in silence for almost a minute, while both of them twist their heads and look in all directions to get a sense of the place where they have just arrived. They know that Gina won't be home for another five minutes and have decided to wait in the car until she does.

From their parking space, they cannot make out the apartment numbers, but Jeremy points his right hand towards five apartments that are connected in one unit and says that it has to be one of those. Suddenly, a middle-aged woman leaves the apartment in the middle and enters the apartment right next door, and it is then that Jeremy realizes that he was pointing his finger in the right direction as he shortly after sees his father leaving the apartment that the middle-aged woman just left. His father carries a handful of trash bags in his left arm and in his right hand there is a lit cigarette which he puffs at in intervals that are shorter than ten seconds. Once he has returned to his apartment door, he puffs at the cigarette at even shorter intervals and once he's done, he hides the stub in a beer bottle which he hides beneath a lantern. Two seconds later, Johnny enters the apartment, and Jeremy looks at his mother who looks as if she has just seen a ghost.

"Are you alright, Mom?" Jeremy says and decides not to wait for an answer which obviously isn't coming. "It doesn't have to be whatever you think it is. There can be a ton of reasons why his neighbor visits him."

"Sure, you're right about that," Alicia says, and tries to convince herself that her son is right; the woman could have been in her ex-husband's apartment to borrow an egg or a screwdriver, or maybe she was picking up something that Johnny had borrowed from her. It's also possible that she was there to give him a package which she had accepted when he wasn't home just as well as it's possible that the middle-aged woman was in his apartment because she's the chairwoman of the local homeowners' association and was there to share important information about the complex. And, even if they have just witnessed the ending of a social visit, that doesn't mean that it was a sexual visit. Maybe Johnny is just befriending his new neighbor in a totally platonic way because he'll otherwise feel lonely, since Gina probably doesn't spend as much time in the apartment as Jeremy does in their house. "I could start all sorts of speculations and imagination, but you're right—it's probably nothing; she's probably nobody."

"Besides, Gina has just texted me. She's here now." The moment Jeremy says that, Alicia spots her daughter at the other end of the parking lot and, for the time being, is able to forget what she has just seen. She gets out of the car to walk straight to her daughter and give her a hug. Jeremy also hugs his sister, the three of them wrapping their arms around each other in what is almost a group hug, and then they approach the apartment.

Once inside, Johnny greets them by giving both of his kids a hug, and since he doesn't know whether to give Alicia a hug or a handshake, he ends up doing something in between, which makes for an awkward beginning to their afternoon rendezvous, but aside from that the next hour passes in a relatively normal and relaxed way; the guided tour of the apartment, as Gina jokingly calls it, takes less than two minutes since the place is so tiny. After that, both Johnny and Gina share what it's like for them to live there, whereupon Alicia and Jeremy tell their hosts what they have been up to in recent weeks, and then the four of them dive further into a polite, but somewhat trivial, conversation.

As Alicia and Jeremy get ready to leave—they had decided beforehand that they would only stay about an hour—Alicia excuses herself to the bathroom and, while sitting on the toilet, notices strands of female hair in the shower stall and makeup stains on the hand shower on the slide rail. She immediately concludes that a female taking showers in her ex-husband's apartment is more than just a visitor and considers asking about the woman who left the apartment right before they got there.

Alicia is convinced that Johnny is dating this woman, and even begins wondering whether he started dating her before the divorce, and if he has moved there to be as close to her as possible; essentially, they're living so close to each other that living together would be a matter of tearing down the wall between his and her apartment, thereby creating one large apartment instead of two tiny apartments. She leaves the bathroom imagining what the place will look like once the turning-two-apartments-into-one project is done. It's not until she sees her daughter that Alicia realizes that the strand of hair and the make-up stains might be hers, but then she questions whether the color of the hair in the sink matches Gina's hair color, and even goes so far as to return to the bathroom—her children give her a weird glance when she claims that she has forgotten something in there—only to arrive at the conclusion that the hair in the sink is actually the exact same color as her daughter's hair. This realization momentarily appeases Alicia and she's able to say goodbye to both Gina and Johnny without further ado.

On their way back home, Jeremy's eyes are glued to his iPhone, so he doesn't notice his mother's emotional distress. Alicia finds herself engaged in an inner monologue in which she again repeats that the woman they saw right before entering Johnny and Gina's apartment is just a strange woman; a nobody, an insignificant and inconsequential person who doesn't have anything to do with her ex-husband. She was there for some random reason, and he is, after all, allowed to have female visitors. Technically, he's allowed to do whatever he wants, she reminds herself, while at the same time thinking that if he were dating someone, she would consider it *too early*.

Once home, Jeremy and Alicia spend a couple of minutes talking about the afternoon. Jeremy thinks they have had a good time and wouldn't mind going again soon, and his mother mumbles that she agrees, although the only thing she can focus on is her repeated and continued attempt to convince herself that Johnny isn't dating the strange woman. She notices that her mind begins to play tricks on her; it has been less than an hour since she convinced herself that the hair in the sink was Gina's hair but now the voice inside of her tells her that this might not be the case after all; was the hair in the sink not slightly darker than Gina's hair? There's no way she can check it again and the more she asks herself this question the more she ends up believing that her previous assumption was false; the hair in the sink does indeed come from another woman, and as soon as she concludes that, she quickly establishes that the other woman is the one next door, and the only possible explanation as to why her hair is in her ex-husband's sink is that they have been showering together, because if she wanted to shower by herself, she might as well just have gone to her own place to do that. Before she knows it, Alicia pictures how steam fills the shower and the glass doors become foggy, and the shapes inside the shower stall are blurry, but not so blurry that her mind cannot create an image of her ex-husband sliding his dick into his neighbor in an upright position while the water cascades onto their bodies.

Alicia's train of thought is interrupted by her son, who lets her know that he's going out. She forgets to ask him where he's going and when he will be back, but as soon as he has left the house she pours herself a drink and decides that imagining herself having sex is probably better for her mental health than imagining her ex-husband having sex, so her mind takes her back to that New York night a few weeks ago when she found herself in the arms of Isaiah, the firefighter who set her loins on fire.

She clearly remembers the night—and the morning—they spent together, and it's very easy for her mind to recreate similar images, and she soon begins touching herself and, in a twinkling, brings herself to an orgasm. She finishes her drink and, while pouring herself another, wonders what it would be like to meet Isaiah again. She reaches for her phone and scrolls through her contacts: Ian, Ibrahim, Imani, Iris, Isabel, and ISAIAH. As soon as she sees his name she remembers; they did exchange numbers before she left and they did talk about seeing each other again someday, and now, while finishing her drink, Alicia begins typing a message: *Hi Isaiah. Hope all is well in NYC. I might be going there in a couple of weeks and was thinking maybe we could meet up. Let me know if you're up for it. All the best, Alicia.*

She reads the message a couple of times and decides that she likes it; it's a bit frisky perhaps, but not over-the-top, and she also likes its succinctness. Alicia considers sending the message, but then Jeremy returns to the house and as he joins her in the living room, she ends up deleting those thirty-nine frisky words and decides to make herself a cup of coffee instead.

Meanwhile, on the opposite side of the river, Johnny is dozing off on the couch when the buzzing of his phone wakes him. He considers ignoring it but his curiosity gets the better of him, as he's not used to getting text messages this late. He sees Janet's name on the screen and becomes increasingly excited as he immediately imagines that she's asking if he wants to come over and his mind instantly concludes that this is finally proof that they are way past that first awkward meeting a few weeks ago; her stopping by earlier today was her way of saying that she has succumbed to his charm.

Now, she has probably had a couple of drinks and in less than an hour his celibacy period will come to an end. He opens the message but has to read it twice before he understands it.

Hi Johnny. Sorry for bothering you this late. Hope I'm not waking you up. I don't mean to sound like a prude, but I have to tell you that your flirtatious comments are a bit too much for me. I like you, and I'm sure we will be great neighbors, but I'll level with you and be honest: I'm not interested in anything romantic between the two of us, so I'm hoping you can tone the flirting down a bit. Thanks, neighbor. Have a good night. Janet. PS: I left the measuring tape that I borrowed outside your door.

Johnny is taken aback by the message and is only able to get up from the couch because he really must take a piss. He stares at himself in the bathroom mirror for a while and the face that stares back at him convinces him that he must have somehow misunderstood the message, so he returns to the living room and reads it again before realizing that there's really not that much to misunderstand.

He walks around in circles while considering his three options: he can ignore the message, he can text her back and tell her that she must have misread him since he's not interested in her, or he can text her back and offer some sort of apology and let her know that he will lessen the flirting.

He chooses the last option and as soon as he has pressed the send button he goes to bed, and, despite not being able to fall asleep, he decides not to get his phone, which he has deliberately left in the kitchen.

He turns on the TV and the news of Trump's recent stops on his campaign trail, Arizona Thursday, Nevada Friday, Salt Lake City tonight, help him simmer down and eventually he's able to fall asleep because he can ignore the fact that he was just rejected and instead focus on the fact that he believes that Trump will be elected.

Chapter ten
312 vs. 226

"It's in the bag," Johnny tells his daughter, and then he gets a beer and makes a drink for Gina, although she hasn't specifically asked for one. "We can raise a toast and mark the occasion," he says as he returns to the living room. It's November 5, and Trump is projected by the news to have won the battleground states of Pennsylvania, Wisconsin, Michigan, North Carolina, and Georgia, which puts him at a total of 291 electoral votes and he can triumphantly raise his arms even though the two remaining swing states, Arizona and Nevada, haven't counted all the votes yet.

As the counting continues throughout the country, it becomes increasingly obvious that Trump has not only defeated Kamala Harris, but he has also done it in a much more convincing way than most people would have thought. The reporters are no longer talking about the fact that the votes that need to be counted are the ones from the major cities, which tend to be mainly Democratic, making them argue that maybe it isn't over yet for Harris. Instead, they are beginning to state the truth that is slowly unfolding in front of the eyes of the American people: Donald Trump will be the 47th president of The United States of America and he will find his way into the history books as the first and only president since Grover Cleveland to be elected to nonconsecutive terms.

"Congratulations, Dad," Gina says and gives him a hug. "Are you surprised?"

"No, I'm not surprised that he won," Johnny says and takes two sips of his beer. "But I'm a bit surprised that he won this big, although opinion polls do tend to underestimate Trump. I can't wait for all the results to roll in and find out exactly how much he wiped the floor with her." He takes two more sips and finishes his beer before Gina has even started her drink, and then asks her if the result comes as a surprise to her.

"Honestly, I didn't know what to expect. Most of my friends believed that Harris would win, so I guess I've been influenced by them and was starting to believe the same thing. But it's my first election as a voter, and I haven't followed the race that closely, so I don't think I could have been surprised regardless of the outcome."

"So, what are your friends saying now?" Johnny makes sure to try to sound as if his question comes from some sort of concern, or at least a genuine interest in her circle of friends. It will be difficult for him not to come across as slightly gleeful towards anyone who has voted for Kamala Harris, but there's no reason to let his daughter know that he thinks her friends got what they deserved.

"Well, they're just posting stuff. TikTok videos with sad-face-filters. Lamenting Instagram reels. Things like that. It seems that they're shocked. As if they hadn't seen it coming at all and still don't understand how Trump could win."

"Do you understand it?"

"Sort of. I get that most people like Trump's view on immigration and stuff. But there are probably many things that I don't understand."

"Do you want me to explain it to you?"

"Go ahead." Gina pauses for a couple of seconds. "But keep it fairly short. I've been sitting on this couch for four hours now. I'm not gonna stay for long."

"Well, like you said, immigration is a huge factor. People obviously have a point when they say that Trump talks about immigrants in a way that is too racist and derogatory, but voting for him doesn't make one a racist. Voting for him doesn't make *you* a racist either, and don't let any of your friends make you think that." Johnny doesn't know if he's pushing it a bit too far with the final comment, but Gina interrupts him before he can even begin regretting it.

"I think most of them don't care about my Trump support, but I have been getting some comments about it, and sometimes, even though they don't say anything, there's this weird vibe when I tell my friends that I'm voting for Trump."

"Are you the only one in your circle of friends, who voted for him?"

"I know for sure that one other girl voted for him, and a couple of the guys considered voting for him as well, but I'm not sure if they ended up going to the polling place or if they stayed at home. But all the ones you know, the ones who've been coming to our house, Stacy, Linsey, Elizabeth, Sophia and Amelia, they are all Democrats."

"That doesn't really surprise me. They're young, they're about to begin college, and we're a Democratic state. Anyway, I was talking about immigration and here's the thing, honey: even though I think Trump's rhetoric is too much at times and immigrants are certainly not as dangerous as he says, I still understand why people think he's better at solving the situation at the border. As much as I'd love to spread my arms and announce that everyone is still welcome here, we are an immigration country after all, the fact of the matter is that the Biden administration has handled the border crisis miserably; even for a nation of immigrants there are limits. There's a limit when it comes to the number of immigrants we can let into this country. Springfield in Ohio is a good example, for instance."

"That's the city where he said that the immigrants were eating the dogs and the cats, right?"

"Exactly. We also talked a bit about it after the debate in September. It's a stupid thing to say, of course, since they're obviously not. So, it's another one of his lies, but it's not a lie to claim that it's challenging for a city with a population of less than sixty thousand residents to bid welcome to more than twenty thousand immigrants. For instance, there are far more car crashes in Springfield now, because the Haitians don't know the traffic laws. And if you need to go to the doctor or a hospital, the line is much longer than what it used to be, 'cause there are all these extra clients, but no extra doctors, or at least not enough extra doctors, and the immigrants need to bring an interpreter when they talk to a doctor so what would otherwise have been a fifteen minutes' session now takes an hour." Johnny pauses and looks at his daughter's drink and doesn't even have to comment on the fact that she hasn't touched it before she asks him if he wants it, and two seconds later he tastes it for the first time. "My point is, Gina, Trump can say whatever he wants about immigrants, and a lot of people, real people who have experienced real problems with immigrants, are going to listen to him. They probably don't like his choice of words either, but they trust him more than they trust the Democrats when it comes to fixing the problems at the border."

"That's a good point. I don't really have that much of an opinion about the immigration thing, but that's probably because we don't have a lot of immigrants around here, so I don't see the problems firsthand."

"No, our town is almost as white as a sheet of paper. But I'll tell you what else made Trump president again, 'cause this is something you do feel firsthand. Do you know what it is?"

"The economy?"

"Exactly, perhaps even more so than the issue of immigration. Have you heard Harris or Biden or any other Democrat say anything about the economy?"

"A bit. I have seen some graphs; something about growth and the stock market moving in the right direction and low unemployment rates. I think I've even heard Biden or Harris say that the unemployment rate was the lowest ever."

"The lowest ever is probably stretching it a bit, but it has been below four percent for a long time, which is quite remarkable. And you're right about the fact that they show a lot of graphs all the time. But you know what, honey, graphs are one thing; what people experience in real life is something else completely and sixty percent of Americans live from paycheck to paycheck. Have you heard that expression?"

Gina is becoming a bit bored but ventures a guess. "Something about only being able to buy the very necessities?" She checks the time on her phone, thereby discreetly letting her father know that he doesn't have to talk at length about the economic pain that is felt by so many of their countrymen and to a certain extent by himself after the divorce.

"Exactly. They can't pay their bills until the next paycheck arrives. It's impossible for these people to save up as much as a dollar, and they're extremely vulnerable when it comes to the increases in prices. We can put aside our concerns about immigration when we want to, and we can do the same with our concerns about abortion rights and the wars around the world, but the concerns that we have about the economy are tormenting us every single day; every time we go the supermarket, or put gasoline in the car, or pay a bill, it's a reminder that we don't have as much money as we used to. Those plastic cards in our wallets are a symbol of the opposite of what they're supposed to symbolize; they are supposed to denote spending power, but they don't; they just remind us that if I buy a steak today then I have bought the one steak that I can afford this month."

"You started out saying *them*, but now you're saying *we*—do you live from paycheck to paycheck, Dad?" Gina is no longer as bored as she was a couple of minutes ago.

"I don't. You don't have to worry about me or us. We'll get by and even if Harris had won the election, we would have made ends meet. But I feel certain that it's gonna be easier for us now that Trump is reelected. And if I were to single out one thing that has led to the reelection of Trump, this is it: most people were better off during Trump's first presidency than they have been during the past four years. A couple of years ago the inflation was through the roof and, while it's better now, I don't think people trusted Harris to keep the inflation under control." Johnny looks closely at his daughter to see if he still has her attention before continuing. "You see, my dear, Harris paid the price for the fact that Biden has made us all pay such a high price on everything from gasoline to food to detergent to clothes to you-name-it. Bidenomics has made so many people feel like they don't have a dime to their names, and she should have done much more to make sure that her name didn't go hand in hand with Biden's name." He finishes his drink, which used to be hers, and as he goes into the kitchen for one more beer, he asks her if she wants one despite being almost certain that she will decline.

Just as expected, Gina tells her father that her election day is over, as she's going to Liam's place, and while opening his next beer, Johnny whispers to himself that the Democrats should shove their graphs about the economy up their asses. He continues to piss and moan about Biden and Harris, and it's not until Gina asks him if he's talking to her that he realizes that he wasn't whispering as silently as he thought. He assures her that he was just talking to himself and as soon as they have said their goodbyes, he tells himself that he's about to have one of those nights when one beer takes the next; it's been a while since he has had one such night and for once he has something to celebrate.

Two hours later Johnny is sauced and decides that it will make sense to reach out to Alicia. He hasn't heard from his ex-wife since two months ago when she and Jeremy visited, and while that might be normal in a situation like theirs, he has, from time to time, thought about contacting her because he hopes that they can someday reestablish some sort of relationship.

However, it's been difficult to come up with an approach; texting her out of the blue would come across as a bit peculiar and he has been worried about how she would react. He has thought about congratulating her on her birthday, which is in a month, but now figures that the election gives him a reason to move faster. A Harris victory would have been better in this case; he even wonders if it would have made it easier for her to forgive him, but at the same time the Trump victory gives him a reason to empathize with her, so he grabs the phone and starts typing:

Dear Alicia. I hope all is well on your end. I just wanted to reach out, for no particular reason. Obviously, you've been watching the election all day and all night and I understand that you're of course disappointed with the outcome. I hope you'll shrug it off as soon as possible. All the best, Johnny.

Because he's drunk he doesn't spend time considering whether or not he should press the send button and as soon as he's done that, he reads the message again, convincing himself that there's nothing in it that he will regret; it's polite and empathetic and it would be easy for her to answer.

At the same time, it's not a message which requires an answer, so that option is left open if she prefers to extend the period of radio silence. A perfect message, he thinks, before passing out on the couch.

*

Trump's victory has been known for some hours, but James still wanders around in the house with a tense posture, a flushed face, and an intense stare, and when Alicia looks closely at him, she also notices that he's clenching his fists from time to time during the conversation. James is on the phone and Alicia can tell that it's his sister on the other end of the line.

She's been a Democrat her whole life, and will most likely remain one, but she's not a die-hard Democrat like her brother. Despite the fact that Alicia is not as such eavesdropping on their conversation, she has gathered that her father and her aunt are not exactly seeing eye to eye on the war in Ukraine.

Alicia cannot make out all her aunt's words but, based on what her father says, she can conclude that her aunt believes that the fact that Trump has more than suggested that he will withdraw US support for Ukraine in the war with Russia is not only a bad thing. By now, James is making himself a cup of coffee so his phone is on the table, and it is put on speaker, making it possible for everyone in the kitchen to hear both sides of the conversation, and James is shaking his head in frustration as his sister's words fill up the room: "I know that Ukrainians fear that Trump will force them to give up land occupied by Russia in exchange for ending the war, and I'm not saying that that would be an ideal solution. I'm just saying it might be the lesser of two evils. It's terrible if they have to give up territory to an invading country led by a modern-day dictator, but the alternative, Harris' alternative, is probably just to continue to support Ukraine in a way which makes sure that they don't lose the war but doesn't enable them to win it either. The war might go on for years then, so think of all the lives that will be spared if the war comes to an end." Since James doesn't say anything, his sister carries on.

"Some even argue that Trump is in a perfect position to bring the war to an end; he can threaten Zelenskyj by saying that he will cut the support, but he can also threaten Putin by saying that he will take a tougher stance against Russia and support Ukraine more than the Biden-Harris administration has."

By now James is done making his coffee and interrupts his sister to let her know that he thinks that Trump is a brute who just likes to rub shoulders with other brutes, and that no matter how he solves this war it will be done hastily and recklessly. He goes on to explain that the European countries are the United States' most important allies and that it is a duty to help them in Ukraine's heroic war against the enemy from the East. Following this, he condescendingly tells her that if she had studied her history, she would know that the European allies, particularly France and Great Britain, failed to stop Hitler although it would have been relatively easy to do so, and the result of not doing that was fifty-five million deaths, and, according to Alicia's father, the situation in Ukraine can be compared to this.

"You can talk about appeasement as much as you like," James' sister says, obviously thinking that it's now her turn to interrupt, and she uses the word appeasement just to let her brother know that she *has* studied her history. "It doesn't change the fact that I think we need to get less involved in foreign conflicts, especially this one. Even if I used all my fingers and all my toes, I would come up short if I were to count how many wars we've been involved with since World War Two. Europe needs to up their military game and not count on us to be their guard dog and they have to pay more as well; some European countries provide very little financial aid to Ukraine despite the fact that the war is right in their backyard. I'm just saying I don't understand why we should pay so much when they pay so little." She pauses before saying the one thing that she knows will make her brother feel like she's sticking a knife into him: "And the voters don't understand that either; you gotta admit that."

James avoids commenting on his sister's final words and instead talks about how Trump is unpredictable and how no one really knows what will happen next. For once, the siblings seem to agree on something and finish the conversation on friendly terms. Alicia's father joins the rest of the family at the dining table. He has a look of resignation on his face and mumbles something about his sister almost sounding like a Republican before he begins talking to the others. "Maybe we just have to face that Harris wasn't the right candidate. It might be too early to analyze the entire thing, but it looks like none of the voter groups really stepped up to the plate for Harris."

"What do you think she did wrong?" Jeremy asks.

"Well, a lot of it is not really something you can blame her for. Biden should've stepped down much earlier. He was supposed to be a one-term president before he suddenly decided to run again. Harris only had one hundred and seven days to campaign, so there are probably a lot of voters out there who don't know her and maybe things would have turned out differently if she'd had more time."

"Maybe, but still she could've used those one hundred and seven days more wisely," Alicia's mother says. She knows that her husband might think she's nit-picking but continues. "She should've done more to distance herself from Biden. I know she wanted to come across as loyal to him, but I don't think that was the right strategy." James looks quizzically at his wife and is just about to interrupt before she continues in a tone which becomes increasingly stern. "Come on, James, we talked about this. There's no need to pretend like she's a good campaigner. She's not; and do you remember what she said when the host of ABC's The View asked her if she would've done anything differently from Joe Biden?" James is so taken aback by the austerity of his wife's tone that he fails to answer her question, which makes her do it herself. "'Nothing comes to mind'" is what she said. She became the new face on Bidenomics, and she became the symbol of everything else that people think Biden handled poorly, when she instead should've made sure not to become synonymous with him."

"I guess we just have to face that we lost," Alicia says, before indirectly telling her parents not to start arguing about the reasons behind the defeat: "Today is too soon to start analyzing things."

"You're right," her father says. "We've lost before, and we'll overcome this crisis as well. At least we have plenty of time to go back to the drawing board and make a good plan for the next election." James tries to make an optimistic smile, but his eyes tell everyone that though he has lived through the defeats of plenty of Democratic candidates—Hillary Clinton in 2016, John Kerry in 2004, Al Gore in 2000, Michael Dukakis in 1988, Walter Mondale in 1984, Jimmy Carter in 1980, George McGovern in 1972, Hubert Humphrey in 1968 and Adlai Stevenson in 1956 and 1952—Harris' downfall torments him in a way that he hasn't experienced before; even Mondale's 13 vs. 525 defeat wasn't as bad as this.

James sits back in his chair and feels as if gravity is pulling him down as he contemplates the idea that the Democratic Party, his party, his family's party, his street's party, his city's party, his state's party, is scattered on the floor—like a puzzle broken by the fall—and no matter where you look you cannot find a person who appears to be able to put the puzzle back together. "So let's call it a night. It looks like it's going to be a 312 vs. 226 Trump victory, and it's getting late and we all need some sleep," he says, and shortly after Alicia and Jeremy are on their way home.

Once they are at home, Jeremy goes straight to bed, and Alicia checks her phone for the first time in a few hours. She reads the message from Johnny and immediately thinks that this was just what she needed for the night to take a turn from bad to worse. She rereads the message and tries to tell herself that there's nothing to be upset about; his choice of words is polite, and he does not in any way gloat about Trump's victory, although she knows for sure that he also sees it as *his* victory. As she keeps staring at the little screen, she tells herself that there's nothing to be mad about, but then she looks up and thinks that there's everything to be mad about; she looks at the wall above the TV and remembers how it used to be filled with pictures of the four of them.

She particularly remembers the picture of them in front of a Best Western hotel just outside Baltimore, a picture that was taken in the summer of 2012, while they were making a pit stop on their way to Florida. She then notices how the wall shows an outline of where the picture used to hang, as the paint around it has faded over the years, while the area beneath the picture remains preserved. It was her favorite picture of their family, and though she told herself every summer that she had to replace it with a newer picture, she knew she was never going to do that.

Over the years, when Alicia felt their marriage wasn't going too well, she would look at this picture and remind herself that this was what they were fighting for. In the photo, Johnny was lifting Jeremy from the ground with his right arm and his left arm was wrapped around Alicia, who was laughing because Gina was tickling her stomach. All four faces displayed expansive smiles and laughter that made the eyes crinkle, and the warm, natural light enhanced the feeling of exaltation. Not once following the summer of 2012 did they manage to get a picture that so perfectly showed the family that they wanted to be, so the picture stayed on the wall for the next twelve years, until seven months ago when Alicia tore it down and threw it in the trash in a fit of rage. Now, the faded silhouette on the wall reminds her that they never became the family in the picture and it's too late to try to become that now; her lying, cheating, deceiving, fucking husband took away the last hope that was lingering inside of her, and the last thing she needs tonight is a message on the phone which reminds her of his existence.

Alicia pours herself a drink as she contemplates which is worse: having had a husband who is a liar and a cheater, or getting a president who is the same? She spends fifteen minutes pondering this question and also imagines Johnny celebrating Trump's victory with the woman next door, whom Alicia is certain her ex-husband is dating on a regular basis now; he has a new girlfriend, he has the president that he wants once again, and he even has one of her children living under his roof. She feels her blood boiling more and more but then she thinks about the message to Isaiah that she wrote and deleted a few weeks ago. She has been thinking about it on and off for the past weeks and, since she remembers it clearly, it takes her less than twenty seconds to type it again.

Hi Isaiah. Hope all is well in NYC. I might be going there in a couple of weeks and was thinking maybe we could meet up. Let me know if you are up for it. All the best, Alicia.

She looks at the words for another twenty seconds and then deletes five words—*in a couple of weeks*—and sends it before going to the kitchen and pouring herself another drink. Once she returns to the living room, she sees that he has already texted her back; he's up for it and tells her that he's at a party and asks her if she means going to New York tonight, in which case he assures her that they could certainly meet up. Alicia spends ten seconds contemplating the idea that he might be a Republican since he's at a party tonight, but quickly decides that the fact that he has a dick is what matters in this situation. She checks her Moovit app which tells her that the next train bound for New York city is also the last train until dawn, and it leaves in fifteen minutes, so she finishes her drink in no time, makes another and pours it into her shaker bottle, which is the first container that she can find, and then she places a Post-it note on the fridge which tells Jeremy that she has to leave for work early.

She makes it to the train just in time and as soon as she's onboard she texts Isaiah that she will be in New York in about an hour and a half. Afterwards, she doesn't put the phone down but instead scrolls through videos and begins looking at the sex-video of herself with Isaiah that they recorded on the night of their first and, so far, only encounter. She hasn't watched it since she left New York that day, but as soon as she presses the play button her body is taken back to that night; she can almost feel and taste him, and had it not been for the presence of a few other passengers she might have started touching herself.

After a few minutes Alicia looks up and notices two giggling teenage girls sitting close to her and it dawns on her that although the sound on her phone is very low, she hasn't muted the video so her phone is not entirely silent, and the girls might be laughing at the sounds from it. While this doesn't bother Alicia, she still stops watching the video and instead focuses on finishing her drink and it's not until she's close to Grand Central Terminal that it hits her that Isaiah hasn't answered her text message. She panics a bit and starts considering whether she should just stay on the train, which will be going in the opposite direction shortly and could have her back in Cold Spring in less than two hours, but then her phone makes the short, xylophone-like *ding* sound and saves her from having to worry any further.

Great. I'm no longer at the party. Just got back to my apartment but stop by if you're up for an afterparty.

The message surprises Alicia a bit and she would have preferred to meet up with Isaiah at a bar before going to his place but quickly decides that there's no need to play hard to get—since she's so obviously the exact opposite at this very moment—so she immediately lets him know that she's certainly up for an afterparty and ten minutes later she's in a taxi which takes her straight to his place.

Isaiah greets her with a warm hug and a cold drink and even though they have plenty of things to talk about—their last encounter, what they have been up to since then, what Alicia is suddenly doing in New York in the middle of the night, work, the election and whatnot—they are in his bedroom less than fifteen minutes after she walked into his living room. Before they begin to rip each other's clothes off, Alicia prepares her phone by finding her contacts and scrolling down to Johnny's name, whereupon she places the phone very close to her in the bed so that she can discreetly call up her ex-husband when the timing is just right.

The foreplay is over in no time, and it's difficult for her to enjoy the sex because she's focused on her revenge plan, but fortunately she doesn't have to wait very long; they're less than five minutes into the intercourse before the beautiful, black specimen on top of her is panting like a madman and without him noticing she presses the green-circled call button on her phone and as soon as she hears Johnny's confused voice she begins to grasp and groan as much as Isaiah. Alicia makes sure that her moans are built up in a steady rhythm, while at the same time becoming deeper and more guttural, before finally releasing a wild, primal cry, which is very easy for her, as she's faked orgasms plenty of times in past years. Since Alicia can still detect her ex-husband's voice below the pillow under which her phone is hidden, she can now let her guard down and let Isaiah bring her to an orgasm which there's nothing fake about. Shortly after, once her breathing has slowed and her heartbeat has returned to a normal rhythm, she looks at her phone; the call is disconnected at this point and before falling asleep Alicia asks herself if she's now one step closer to letting bygones be bygones.

The end